"I haven't decided if I'm going to help you or not."

"Oh, you're going to help me," Beau said. His evocative body heat reached out to caress her.

"And what makes you so sure of that?" Peyton took a step back. She hated him for the way he had branded her with his touch, for leaving an indelible mark on her that she realized now no amount of time could have erased.

"Why am I sure? Because you're curious. Because you've spent many sleepless nights wondering if I was really guilty or not. I think you've spent many nights thinking about me and what we shared. I know I have."

"You're wrong. I never thought about you at all," she replied defiantly...angrily. "The minute I heard about the details of the crime, I stopped thinking about you."

He laughed, the low, seductive tone making her heart beat a little faster. Could he hear the frantic beat of her heart? Was he aware of how deeply she was affected just by talking to him?

UNSOLVED BAYOU MURDER

New York Times Bestselling Author
CARLA CASSIDY

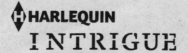

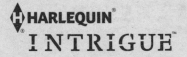

HARLEQUIN®

INTRIGUE™

Recycling programs
for this product may
not exist in your area.

ISBN-13: 978-1-335-59133-3

Unsolved Bayou Murder

Copyright © 2023 by Carla Bracale

For questions and comments about the quality of this book, please contact us at CustomerService@Harlequin.com.

Harlequin Enterprises ULC
22 Adelaide St. West, 41st Floor
Toronto, Ontario M5H 4E3, Canada
www.Harlequin.com

Printed in U.S.A.

Carla Cassidy is an award-winning, *New York Times* bestselling author who has written over 170 books, including 150 for Harlequin. She has won the Centennial Award from Romance Writers of America. Most recently she won the 2019 Write Touch Readers' Award for her Harlequin Intrigue title *Desperate Strangers*. Carla believes the only thing better than curling up with a good book is sitting down at the computer with a good story to write.

Books by Carla Cassidy

Harlequin Intrigue

The Swamp Slayings

Unsolved Bayou Murder

Kings of Coyote Creek

Closing in on the Cowboy
Revenge on the Ranch
Gunsmoke in the Grassland

Desperate Strangers
Desperate Intentions
Desperate Measures
Stalked in the Night
Stalker in the Shadows

Scene of the Crime

Scene of the Crime: Deadman's Bluff
Scene of the Crime: Return to Bachelor Moon
Scene of the Crime: Return to Mystic Lake
Scene of the Crime: Baton Rouge
Scene of the Crime: Killer Cove
Scene of the Crime: Who Killed Shelly Sinclair?
Scene of the Crime: Means and Motive

Visit the Author Profile page at Harlequin.com.

CAST OF CHARACTERS

Peyton LaCroix—As a defense attorney, was she helping an innocent man, or was Beau the cold-blooded killer she'd believed he was for the past fifteen years?

Beau Boudreau—He knew he was an innocent man. Now he needed Peyton's help to prove it.

Jackson Fortier—Had Peyton's friend committed the ultimate sin in an effort to put Beau behind bars?

Thomas Gravois—Had the chief of police covered up a crime to protect one of his own?

Gator Broussard—What exactly did the old man living in the swamp know?

Chapter One

Peyton LaCroix tapped her pencil on her desk and stared outside her office window. From this vantage point she could see up and down the main street of Black Bayou. The little town looked tired, with storefronts that were weathered and old. Heat shimmered up from the sidewalks, not uncommon for mid-July in Louisiana.

Above the buildings and in the distance, tall, bald cypress trees rose up and dripped with Spanish moss. Along with the cypress trees there were also water tupelos and black gum trees. They were a constant reminder of the swamp that half surrounded the small town.

The swamp and the people who lived there had always fascinated Peyton. The dark, murky waters with all the strange vegetation held both a sense of mystery and a faint hint of danger.

She'd found the people who came from the swamp to be proud and passionate, hardworking and generally law-abiding. Except for one. Her pencil lead suddenly snapped.

Her office door flew open and Kylie Bradford entered. "Hey, boss," she said and flopped down in the chair opposite Peyton's desk. "I'm bored."

"That makes two of us," Peyton admitted.

"I'm thinking about going out and committing a crime just so you can defend me."

Peyton laughed. "I'm not *that* bored. However, you would make a good defendant…nothing bad in your background and with your halo of blond hair, blue eyes and angelic features you could definitely charm a jury."

"That's good to know for future purposes," Kylie replied with a grin. "I really came in here to see if you wanted a sandwich or something else to eat. I'm going to run down to Big Larry's for my lunch."

Big Larry's was a sandwich and burger joint a block away from Peyton's office. "I'm really not in the mood for a sandwich, but I would eat a side of his cold pasta salad."

"Then pasta salad it is," Kylie said and stood. Peyton grabbed her purse from under the desk, but Kylie waved her away. "Lunch is on me today. I'll be back in fifteen or twenty minutes."

"Take your time. It's too hot out there to rush," Peyton replied.

When Peyton had opened her law office here in Black Bayou, she'd advertised for an assistant and the twenty-five-year-old, bright and energetic Kylie had answered the ad. She'd hired Kylie and since that time the two had become great friends.

With Kylie gone, Peyton leaned back in her chair and closed her eyes. For the past fifteen years she'd been solely focused on her career as a defense attorney. She had graduated law school early and then had been lucky enough to get a job at a highly respected, busy law firm in Shreveport. During her last three years there she had worked on several high-profile cases that she'd won.

However, a year ago she'd realized she was beyond exhausted by the long hours and frantic pace her work entailed. She had no life outside of work so she'd made the decision that it was time to come home. She had moved back to Black Bayou and bought a small home and the building where she now had her office.

Her home was a cute two-bedroom that was perfect for just her, but her office building needed tons of work to replace rotting boards and repaint the entire building on the outside. The amount of work needed was the reason she'd gotten a good deal on it. Unfortunately, she hadn't yet pulled together all the energy or the funds to start any of the renovations.

She had a healthy retirement fund but so far hadn't been willing to tap into it for the repairs. She'd much rather make the money with her practice, but things had been slow.

At thirty-three years old she was now half-broke, but glad to have a slower pace. She was also ready to start building a personal life for herself. That started tonight. She had another date with Sam Landry, a respected banker she'd seen several times since returning to Black Bayou.

Kylie returned with lunch, and the afternoon hours crept by. The last case Peyton had worked had wrapped up the week before. A teenage boy from the swamp had been caught spray-painting the side of a building owned by a prominent family, and that family wanted the book thrown at the boy. The district attorney had overcharged the kid, and his distraught parents had come to Peyton for help.

At the bench trial, Peyton had argued passionately for a reduction of charges. She made a case for probation and community service and thankfully, the judge had agreed with her.

His parents had been thrilled, but Peyton also knew they were not a moneyed family so she'd cut her fees in half, and Kylie had set up a payment plan for them.

It was just after three when Kylie came back through her office door. She shut the door behind her. "There is a totally hot guy out there in the waiting room. I've never seen him before and he wouldn't give me his name but he insists he wants to see you."

"Then by all means send him in," Peyton replied. She didn't care how *hot* the guy was, she was just hoping he needed counsel. She could definitely use the work.

Kylie left the room and a moment later *he* stepped over the door's threshold. A loud roar resounded in Peyton's head as she stared at the man who had been her first love…and her first betrayal.

Fifteen years had passed since she'd last seen Beau Boudreau, a man spawned by the swamp…and perhaps the very devil himself. He'd been twenty-one years old the last time she'd seen him. At that time he'd been darkly handsome with a hint of something wild and magnetic.

The years hadn't changed that. If anything, age had chiseled his features, removing anything boyish that had once clung to him. His shoulders were still broad and his hips were slim. His body exuded a sinewy strength. His long black hair was now cut short, and there was something hard and bitter in the depths of his eyes.

He now gazed at her with dark, hooded eyes as he appeared to take in each and every one of her features.

Her pulse immediately quickened as a flash of memories flooded her brain, hot and painful memories she'd spent the past fifteen years trying to forget. The flicker of a kerosene lantern…the pain and then the pleasure of Beau. Finally, the utter heartbreak that had left her scarred forever.

"I didn't know you were out." She finally found her voice.

He walked over to the chair before her desk and sat. He exuded a tightly controlled energy that was both compelling and more than a little bit off-putting. "I got out this morning and got to Black Bayou about an hour ago."

"Why are you here, Beau?" She was grateful her

voice was cool and calm, not reflecting the hundreds of emotions that roared through her.

His lips curved into a sardonic grin as his heated gaze swept over her. "I know how the last fifteen years have treated me. I was curious to see how they'd treated you and I must say, *ma chérie*, they have treated you very well. You are more beautiful than I thought you would be, even more beautiful than I dreamed about. Did you ever think of me while I was away?"

"No…never," she snapped quickly. His wicked grin let her know he didn't believe her. "What are you really doing here? What do you want, Beau?"

The smile disappeared and once again there was a flash of pain…of something bitter in the depths of his eyes. The emotions were only there a moment and then disappeared as his eyes went as dark and enigmatic as the swamp waters. "I want you to help me reinvestigate the murder that sent me away."

She stared at him in stunned surprise. "Beau, you were convicted and you've now served your sentence. Why stir it all up again?" The last thing she wanted was to go back to that place and time when he'd ripped the very heart…the very soul, out of her.

He leaned forward, his gaze so dark, so intense, it threatened to swallow her up whole. "I was innocent when I was convicted, and I'm innocent as I sit here today. We need to find something that will overturn my conviction, something that will prove my innocence to everyone."

He sat back in the chair. "I need you, Peyton. I

don't have much money, but looking at the outside of this building I thought maybe we could barter. I'll do the work on your office in exchange for you helping me to investigate the crime that wrongly put me in prison."

"Beau, this whole thing is absurd," she said.

"It's not absurd. It's a matter of my honor…my reputation. This is about my life, Peyton." The words exploded out of him with a passionate force. He drew in several deep breaths before continuing. "I need this, Peyton. I need you."

"And I need some time to think about all this, Beau," she finally said.

"How much time?"

"I'll let you know my decision sometime tomorrow afternoon."

He stood. "This is important, Peyton. Fifteen years ago a murderer got away with his crime, and that murderer is probably still walking the streets of Black Bayou."

He didn't wait for her reply. He turned and left the office, taking most of the energy in the room with him. Peyton released a shuddery sigh, still shocked by what had just happened.

At that moment Kylie came back into her office and sank down in the chair Beau had just vacated. "So who was that hunky guy?"

"Beau Boudreau."

Kylie frowned. "Why does that name sound so familiar to me?"

"Fifteen years ago he was charged and convicted in the murder of Lacy Dupree, a young woman who was working as a sex worker out of the motel. Apparently, he just got out of prison earlier today." Once again, a rush of emotions tried to gut Peyton.

"Oh yeah, I remember my mom telling me about it when she was warning me about men. So what does he want from you?"

"He wants me to help him reinvestigate the original crime in order to prove his innocence."

"Hmm… I smell money coming in," Kylie said.

"Well, don't. He wants to barter with me. For my help, he'll do the renovations on this building."

"Is he capable of doing that kind of work?" Kylie asked curiously.

Peyton nodded. "Before his conviction, he and Jack Fontenot were partners in creating a construction company. Beau definitely knows his way around all areas of carpentry." It felt odd, talking about Beau when his name hadn't left her lips for so many years.

"I think I'm going to close up shop early today," she said.

"That's right. You have a hot dinner date to get ready for," Kylie replied.

Peyton laughed. "I'm not sure how hot it's going to be, but I'm definitely ready to call it a day, so you're free to leave as well."

Kylie sprang up from her chair. "Then I'm getting out of here before you change your mind."

Minutes later Kylie was gone, the office door

locked, but Peyton remained in her chair as thoughts of Beau swirled around her head.

There had been a time when she'd thought Beau was her future, when she had believed they would be together forever. Her love for him had been fever pitched and all-consuming until the night he'd been arrested for murder.

On that night, after hearing all the ugly details of the crime, her love for him had turned to hatred. She'd recognized him then as not only a heartbreaker, but also the thief of her innocence and the stealer of her dreams.

With his sinful dark eyes and whispered words of love, he'd fooled her completely. She now realized she'd never really recovered from the betrayal.

She finally got up from her chair, grabbed her purse and headed out the front door. She gulped in the hot, sultry air and realized she hadn't drawn a normal breath since Beau had stepped into her office.

She'd told him she'd give him an answer tomorrow, but right now in this moment she didn't know what her answer would be. Could she really go back in time and work with him without losing her very soul?

It would certainly be difficult, especially given the fact that for the past fifteen years in the murder of Lacy Dupree, she'd believed he was guilty as sin.

BEAU RAN THROUGH the swamp, the humid, junglelike air clinging to him like a second skin. *Freedom.* It sang through his veins as the familiar scents of home filled his nose.

Despite the many years away, his feet remembered exactly where to step and when to jump to avoid the alligator-infested water. He'd spent the past fifteen years dreaming of being back here...back home.

He ducked under the Spanish moss that hung from the trees. Insects clicked and whirred, and animals scurried through the thick underbrush as if to protest his presence.

The swamp was in his blood, as was the woman he'd just left. Peyton. All his muscles tightened just thinking about her. And he'd had years to think about her, to remember the scent and taste of her skin, the slide of her nakedness against his and the sweet rapture of making love to her.

She'd been a sweet innocent, something clean and good in his miserable, ugly life. He'd met her when she'd been ten and he'd been thirteen. She'd been sitting on a fallen log deep in the swamp and she was crying.

She'd told him she had run away from home because her parents didn't care about her. All they cared about was the fancy parties they attended. Her plan had been to live in the swamp, but darkness had begun to fall and she was afraid and hopelessly lost.

They had talked for about fifteen minutes and then he had taken her by the hand, led her out of the swamp and walked her home. That had been the beginning of their friendship, a friendship that had blossomed into something deeper…something much hotter as they'd grown up.

For a little over four months they'd been lovers, and memories of those moments when he'd held her in his arms, when his mouth had plied hers with fiery intent, were what had gotten him through the past fifteen years of prison hell.

However, that had been a long time ago and he had no idea what kind of woman she'd become. The only things he knew about her were that she hadn't married and she'd become a criminal defense attorney. He'd learned those things from the one woman who had believed in his innocence, a person who had written to him regularly while he'd been in the slammer.

Marie Boujoulais had escaped the swamp years ago when she'd opened up the Black Bayou Café. Beau's mother had abandoned him when he'd been five years old, leaving Beau to be raised by his cruel alcoholic father. When Beau was ten, Marie had caught him sneaking into her kitchen to steal food.

Rather than shooing him away, she'd sat him at a table and fed him, forming a bond that had lasted through the years. She was the mother he'd never had, the woman who had civilized the little swamp rat he was quickly becoming without any adult guidance.

He'd go see Marie later this evening. What he wanted now was to be home in the three-room shanty where he'd been living with his father before his life had been ripped away from him.

As he got closer, he quickened his pace. Then he saw it...home. The shanty, which was on poles to elevate it over the dark swamp water, was more weatherworn than it had been when he'd left. His footsteps clattered on the wooden bridge that led to the front door.

"Dad!" he yelled as he walked in. The entire place resonated with a yawning emptiness. Dust covered the tabletops and the top of the small potbellied stove that was used for both heating and cooking. It appeared that nobody had been inside the place for years.

He opened the door of his father's bedroom, half expecting his dad to be passed out among the filthy sheets. But nobody was inside the room.

He then went across the plank floor and opened his bedroom door. The room had been ransacked. Clothes were tossed out of the dresser drawers and the small closet. The bedding had been ripped off and now had a home on the floor.

There was no way he believed this was the work of a thief. He was sure his father was the culprit. If he was to guess, the day his father realized Beau wasn't coming home anytime soon, he went through the room looking for any money or valuables he could find to use to buy him more of the cheap gin he loved.

Thankfully, Beau's tool belt and tools were still in the bottom of his closet. For whatever reason, his father had left those alone.

Beau sank down on the edge of the bed. He didn't care about the state of the room. It could be fixed with just a little bit of work. Despite the mess, this room held most of his memories of Peyton.

For just a moment he allowed those memories free rein. He saw her beautiful features in the flicker from a lantern on his nightstand, felt the heat of her body as their naked limbs tangled together. He closed his eyes. If he breathed just right, he could almost smell the lingering scent of her, one of mysterious flowers with a hint of dark spices and a heady dose of woman.

"Beau?"

The deep voice snapped Beau's eyes open and he got up and left the bedroom. "Hey, man." Jack Fontenot grinned at him and pulled him into a bear hug. "I heard there had been a sighting of you in town, so I took a chance that I'd find you here," he said as the hug ended.

Jack had been a big man with a barrel chest when Beau had been locked up. None of that had changed in the years that had passed. He was clad in a pair of black slacks and a short-sleeved button-up blue shirt that emphasized the bright blue of his eyes. Despite Jack's coming from an affluent family in town, the two had been best friends since the time they were thirteen.

Jack had been fascinated by all things swamp and had spent most of his teenage years hanging out at Beau's place, despite his parents' outrage.

Beau now motioned his friend to a seat on the sofa and then Beau sat in the chair facing him. "I got in earlier today. I thought my father might be here, but he isn't."

Jack looked at him somberly. "Nobody told you?"

"Told me what?" Beau asked.

"He's dead, Beau. He died about three months ago. One of his drinking buddies found him dead in the swamp."

Beau wanted to grieve, but it was difficult to grieve for a man who had either beaten him hundreds of times a week or disappeared for long periods. Still, a hint of grief swept through him…the grief for the father he had never had.

"But you look good and fit," Jack said. "I was afraid that you might come back with a big gut after all the carbs they served you."

"I did a lot of exercising in my cell and in the prison's gym whenever I was allowed. How's the business going?" Fifteen years ago, before he went to prison, he and Jack had started their own construction company. At the time Beau went away, they hadn't filed the actual paperwork to make the company official, but they had been working together for about six months. The company had been Beau's dream of making something of himself.

"Terrific. I now have eight men working for me."

"That's good news. I'll be ready to jump back in within a month or so." Surely, a month would give him and Peyton plenty of time to clear his name. "Maybe we could get together sometime next week and you can show me the books."

Beau certainly didn't expect Jack to share the profits with him when he'd been away, but there should be some money for him as a co-owner of the company. Beau just wanted what was fair.

"Sure, we'll talk business next week," Jack replied. "And speaking of business, I need to get back to it. I just wanted to stop in and welcome you home." The two men stood.

"It's damn good to be home," Beau replied. He walked over to the small desk in the room and found a notepad and a pen. "Why don't you give me your cell phone number. I intend to buy a phone sometime tomorrow, but this way once I have a phone, I can put your number into it."

Jack rattled off his number and Beau wrote it down. Minutes later Beau was once again alone. He sank back down in the chair with the pad and pen still in hand.

There were so many things he needed to do in order to reclaim his life. He'd walked out of prison with only several thousand dollars to his name. He'd earned the money by working in the prison laundry room. With that money he needed to buy a cell phone, groceries and new clothing, among other things. He made himself a list of what he needed to take care of and then stood.

It was already getting late in the day and so he'd take care of most of those things tomorrow. But now he was hungry and there was nothing here to eat. He'd go to the café tonight and see Marie.

By the time he left the cabin, twilight had begun to fall and the moon was a half sliver just peeking over the horizon. Fish slapped in the water at the same time the frogs began to croak their deep-throated rhythm. These were the lullabies of the swamp, the lullabies Beau had missed in the concrete cell that had been his home for the past fifteen years.

It took him only ten minutes after he left the swamp to walk to the café. Instead of going through the front door, he went around back and through the alley until he reached the back door of the establishment.

He wasn't ready to face many people right now. In truth, he had no idea how he would be received as a murderer come home. He'd served his time—no, he'd served *somebody else's time*—but he didn't think that would matter with most people. Certainly, most everyone in town hadn't had a problem believing he'd committed a crime of passion and had strangled a woman in the act of erotic asphyxiation.

After all, he was nothing more than an uneducated, uncivilized swamp rat, abandoned by his own mother and raised by a gin-soaked father.

When he reached the back door, he found two young men standing in the alley. They both wore hairnets and they were smoking cigarettes. "I need to talk to Marie," Beau said. "Can one of you go get her for me?"

"Sure," one of them replied. They both dropped their cigarette butts on the ground and went inside.

"This better be good." Marie's French-accented Creole voice rose above the kitchen clatter.

He stepped into the doorway. Marie's dark eyes widened as if she saw a ghost, then she flew toward him and pulled him tight against her ample bosom.

She finally released him and swiped tears from her eyes. "Beau, I wondered if I would stay alive long enough to see you again."

Beau laughed. "Ah, Marie, you are far too wicked for death to come looking for you."

There was no question that she'd aged. Her black hair was now nearly white and her face sported more wrinkles, but her eyes remained the same. The dark depths held a lifetime of misery, a fierce pride and an ancient wisdom.

She laughed and then quickly sobered. "You look thin. Sit." She pointed to a small wooden table shoved into a corner, out of the way of the kitchen staff. "I know you haven't had a good meal since the last time you ate here."

"You've got that right," he said as he sank down at the table.

She shooed several of the line cooks away from the stove and then grabbed a bowl. She dipped him up a liberal serving of her jambalaya and set it in front of him.

She then returned to another stovetop, grabbed a plate and got him a serving of greens and a big hunk of golden cornbread. She placed that plate before him and then sat across from him.

"I know my father is dead," he said.

"Ah, Beau, I didn't have the heart to tell you in a letter. How did you hear?"

"Jack stopped by my place earlier. He told me."

"I'm so sorry for your loss."

He grinned at her. "We both know his death is no loss to me personally. I grieved for him years ago."

She reached out and patted the back of his hand. "God rest his soul. He was certainly a troubled man." She sat back in her chair. "What are your plans now that you're home?" she asked.

"My main goal is to prove my innocence and find out who really killed Lacy."

Marie stared at him for a long moment. "Maybe it's best to just let the dead stay dead. Maybe it would be better for you to look forward instead of back."

"I can't do that, Marie. I want my good name back." He wanted everyone in town to know that he'd been an innocent man convicted of a crime he hadn't committed.

"You'll be stirring up the devil's dust," Marie said, her dark eyes filled with concern.

"I'll dance with the devil himself to find out who really killed Lacy and framed me for the crime," he replied firmly. "This is something I need to do."

He wanted Peyton to know that he hadn't cheated on her. He needed her to know that he was an innocent man. She'd been a fire in his soul, a lust in his veins.

Each night when he'd been in his bunk alone, it had been thoughts and dreams of their passionate lovemaking and their love for each other that had helped him keep his sanity.

Peyton might not know it yet, but he intended to have her in his bed once again.

Chapter Two

"Surely, you aren't really considering helping that murderer." Jackson Fortier stared at Peyton, obviously appalled by what she'd just told him about Beau's visit earlier in the day.

Jackson had been waiting for her on her front porch when she'd come home from her dinner date with Sam. It wasn't unusual for her best friend to pop in at the end of a day.

She and Jackson had bonded together as children at the many parties their parents attended. It was a friendship that had stood the test of time. It had been Jackson's arms that had held her years ago as she'd wept about Beau. He had warned her about getting involved with Beau in the first place.

Jackson's last name held a lot of power. Nothing really got done in Black Bayou unless the Fortier family approved. He was a trust-fund baby who now worked as a real estate developer. Jackson was exceedingly handsome and could be charming to a fault, but there was no hint of that charm on his features at the moment.

He sat across from where Peyton sat on the sofa. He leaned forward, his dark eyes snapping with a simmering fury. "That man has some nerve coming to you for anything. Have you forgotten that he stole all your innocence, all the good you had inside you, and then he trashed it all? He was swamp scum then and now he's a swamp scum ex-con. He's the last man on earth you should get tangled up with again. So please tell me you told him to go to hell."

He leaned back in the chair as Peyton released a deep sigh. "No, I didn't tell him to go to hell."

"So you told him to get the hell out of your office?" Jackson asked.

"Not exactly," she replied. "I told him I'd think about it."

Jackson released a string of curses the likes of which Peyton had never heard from him before. "I can't believe you would even be thinking about helping him. He nearly destroyed you the last time you had any interaction with him."

"If I do decide to help him, it will be strictly business between us."

"Do you really believe you can dance with the devil and not pay a price?" Jackson shook his head.

"He's not the devil," Peyton protested faintly.

"Maybe not, maybe so. What I do know is that man wrapped his necklace around Lacy Dupree's neck and then squeezed the very life out of her."

"He says he's innocent and the killer is still probably out there walking the streets of Black Bayou," she said.

"I've never heard of an ex-con who didn't proclaim his own innocence," he replied with a snort of derision.

Peyton released another deep sigh. "It's getting late, Jackson, and I'm exhausted."

"Of course." He stood and she got up as well. She walked him to the door, where he turned around and gazed at her. "You know I positively adore you, Peyton, and I've always only wanted the very best for you."

"I know that," she replied.

"The best thing you can do for yourself is run as fast and as far as you can away from Beau." He kissed her on the forehead. "Good night, Peyton."

"'Night, Jackson."

Minutes later Peyton was in bed, her mind swirling with everything Jackson had said to her. She knew her friend was right, that she should run as fast and as far as she could from Beau.

But what if he really was an innocent man? A little voice whispered in the back of her head. This was the reason she'd decided to become a criminal defense attorney in the first place…to defend the innocent. So was Beau really an innocent man or was he the monster who had strangled a woman to death?

She finally fell asleep…and into dreams of Beau. In her dream she was in his arms. His bold features were visible in the flicker of a kerosene lantern, and his dark eyes glittered with the hunger of a wild animal.

His hands caressed her nakedness as his mouth plundered hers. Hot…she was on fire and lost in all things Beau. In that moment he owned her—heart, body and soul.

As he entered her, he wrapped his rope necklace with the gold cross around her neck. He pumped into her and as he did, he tightened the necklace around her throat. Faster and faster, he moved against her, into her, and the necklace tightened even more.

"Beau, you're…you're choking me," she finally said with alarm. "Stop…" She reached up to grab the necklace but it was too tight for her to even get her fingers beneath it.

Still, it not only cut into her neck, but also stole her ability to draw a breath. She struggled against him, trying to get free, but he held her tightly in place as he pulled the rope necklace tighter and tighter still.

She couldn't breathe. Her head spun as a blinding dizziness overtook her. She was dying…being strangled to death by the man she loved.

She jerked awake, gasping for air and sobbing. Her heart beat a thousand miles a minute, resounding in her ears like the frantic beat of a Mardi Gras parade drummer gone wild.

She threw off the covers on her bed and got up, the love and then the abject terror of the dream still rocking through her. She went into the adjoining bathroom and flipped on the light, hoping the illumination would chase away the utter darkness of the nightmare.

Half expecting to see a rope imprint around her neck, she stared into the mirror over the sink. Of course, there were no marks on her throat. With a shuddery breath she began to sluice cold water over her face.

Finally, she managed to calm herself down. She went back into her bedroom and sat on the edge of the bed. Had the nightmare been some sort of a warning from the universe? What was she going to tell Beau when he came back in to talk to her? She honestly didn't know.

She finally fell back to sleep, and the next time she awakened it was time to get up and start her day. After showering she stood in front of her closet and pulled out a pair of black slacks and a royal blue blouse that she often got compliments on when she wore it because it perfectly matched her eyes.

At eight forty-five she left her house to drive the five blocks to her office. As she drove, she tried not to think about Beau. She still hadn't made a decision about whether she intended to help him out or not.

With Jackson's warnings and the remnants of the disturbing nightmare still ringing in her head, it was difficult for her to gain any clarity about the matter.

Beau had always been a dark whisper against her skin, a burning flame deep within her. She'd never been able to forget their summer of love…the hot sultry nights when they'd come together with a mindless, wild passion that to date she had never experienced with any other man.

She'd spent what felt like a lifetime hating him. She still hated him for betraying her love with Lacy Dupree. Whether he killed the woman or not, he'd been with her in the motel room where she lived and conducted her business. It had been so difficult to marry the details of the horrible murder to the man she loved.

By nine o'clock she was in her office chair and staring blankly at her computer screen. She started as Kylie opened her door and came in, carrying a coffee cup in hand.

"Morning, boss," she said as she set the coffee on the desk next to Peyton and then sank down in the chair facing the desk.

"Good morning, Kylie." Peyton picked up the cup and took a deep drink of the dark brew. "Mmm, thanks," she said as she returned the cup to her desk.

"Since we don't have anything on the agenda today, I figured I'd work on accounts receivable. We still have a few people who are not honoring the payment plans we set up for them."

"That sounds good to me," Peyton said. "I have some paperwork to do and…" She jumped at the sound of a loud bang outside the building. "What on earth?" She and Kylie both got up, and Kylie followed Peyton to the front door.

Peyton opened the door and there he was. Beau

was clad in jeans and a white T-shirt that showcased his broad shoulders and big biceps. He held a hammer in his hand and as he turned to look at her, his sultry lips slid into a sinful smile.

"Beau, what are you doing?" she asked.

"I thought I'd get started on this place. My plan is to work out here in the mornings, giving you time to work on whatever you need to, and then we'll spend the afternoons working together on what we discussed yesterday," he said.

"I haven't even decided if I'm going to help you out or not," she replied.

He dropped the hammer and sauntered closer to her, invading her personal space with his intense masculinity. His warm body heat reached out to caress her. "Oh, you're going to help me," he said confidently, with a touch of amusement.

"And what makes you so sure of that?" She took a step back from him, irritated by his smooth smile. She hated him for the way he had branded her with his touch, spoiled her for any other man who might try to love her, and for leaving an indelible mark on her that she realized now no amount of time could have erased.

"Why am I sure? Because you're curious. Because you've spent many sleepless nights wondering if I was really guilty or not. I think you've spent many nights thinking about me and what we shared. I know I have."

"You're wrong. I never thought about you at all,"

she replied defiantly…angrily. "The minute I heard about the details of the crime I stopped thinking about you."

He laughed, the low, seductive tone making her heart beat a little faster. Could he hear the frantic beat of her heart? Was he aware of how deeply she was affected just by talking to him?

"Ah, *chérie*, I've never known you to be a liar before, but I see the pulse at the base of your throat is throbbing. It tells me you aren't speaking the truth right now."

She fought the impulse to reach up and cover her throat. And that made her think about the nightmare she'd had the night before. "Okay, I'll help you."

He raised a dark brow. "You will?" For just a moment she saw a flash of vulnerability in his eyes, a vulnerability that held just a touch of hope. "Why have you decided to help me?"

"You're right, I am curious," she replied. "I'm curious to find out if you were really an innocent man or if you're the cheating, lying son of a bitch I've believed you to be all this time."

He smiled again. His gaze bore into hers and then slid downward, lingering pointedly on the thrust of her breasts before sweeping down the length of her and back up again. "Thank you, Peyton. I look forward to working closely with you."

His words, along with his gaze, held a blatant sexuality that swept a wild wave of heat through her. "I'll see you inside this afternoon," she said stiffly.

She turned on her heels and hurried back into the building, half running over Kylie in the process.

She went into her office with Kylie hot on her heels. She sank down behind her desk and Kylie remained standing and looked at her expectantly. "Girl, you've got some explaining to do," Kylie said. "I thought I knew everything there was to know about you, but you missed the part about Beau."

Peyton released a deep sigh. "There isn't that much to tell. When I was eighteen and Beau was twenty-one years old we dated for about four months. Then he was arrested and that was the end of that."

Kylie raised a pale blond eyebrow. "I have a feeling there's way more to the story than that, but I'll get busy on those accounts now."

"Thank you, Kylie."

Alone in her office, Peyton leaned back in her chair and closed her eyes. There was no way to explain to Kylie the overwhelming and abiding love she'd once felt for Beau. There was no way to explain to anyone the white-hot desire, the utterly breathtaking passion of their lovemaking.

There were moments after his arrest that she didn't think she would survive her heartbreak…moments that she could scarcely draw a breath. And now she had invited him back into her life once again.

However, things would be completely different between them this time around. It would be a strictly professional relationship. There was no way she'd let him into her personal life ever again.

He was just a client, and he would never, ever be anything more to her again.

BEAU WORKED ON the front of the building, removing rotten boards until noon, and then he ran home to take a shower. It had felt good to be working again, to know he was going to transform Peyton's building from sad and weathered to something new and inviting.

It was why he'd decided to start the construction company with Jack in the first place. Beau had always enjoyed carpentry and he knew he was good at it and could make a good living at it.

He'd been pleased when he'd broached the idea of a company to Jack, and Jack had immediately gotten on board. Beau was no fool; he knew the Fontenot name would give the company a respectability, a legitimacy, that Beau would never be able to gain on his own.

Beau figured with his hard work and Jack's money and name, there was no way the business wouldn't be successful. From what Jack had told him in their brief conversation, the company had, indeed, become very successful.

However, the construction business wasn't what was on Beau's mind as he made his way back to Peyton's office. He'd been slightly surprised that she had agreed to help him. He knew she must have hated him when he'd been arrested and the sordid details of the crime had come out.

He'd made love to Peyton early in the evening and they had professed their love for each other. Then the next morning he'd been arrested for having kinky sex and killing a sex worker.

He'd never gotten a chance to plead his case with her; instead, he'd been handed over to an overworked public defender who hadn't stood a chance against the aggressive prosecuting attorney whom everyone knew was prejudiced against swamp people. That, coupled with the physical evidence, had put the nail in Beau's coffin.

There had always been a prejudice between the upper crust in the town and the people who lived in the swamp. Swamp people were ignorant, gator-chasing lowlifes who'd steal you blind if you let them get too close.

And yet, they were good enough to scrub your toilets or sweep your floors or cook for your family. Beau had grown up with the taint of the swamp on him, making it easy for people to believe him guilty of the murder.

Even the woman he'd loved had believed him guilty, and that had been a stabbing pain in his soul that even now burned deep inside him. It had been a betrayal he'd never forgotten.

Peyton had known him. She'd known him better than any other human being on the face of the earth. He'd opened himself up to her…been vulnerable with her. Even though he'd known that her upper-crust family would never approve of him, she'd made him believe that their love was strong enough to see them through any obstacle.

Yet, when push came to shove, she'd been like all the others, assuming the worst of him before even giving him a chance to talk to her. And there was a small part inside him that still couldn't get over that particular betrayal.

Now he was depending on her help to clear his name. The irony of the situation wasn't lost on him. But as a criminal defense attorney, she was the best person for the job, and probably the only person who would even consider doing this for him.

He made one quick stop before heading back to Peyton's place. By that time, it was well after one. He finally reached her building and pulled open the front door. The receptionist desk was staffed by the same young blonde who had let him in the day before.

She popped up from her desk with a smile. "We haven't been officially introduced," she said. "I'm Kylie Bradford, Peyton's assistant, and I know you're Beau Boudreau."

"It's nice to meet you, Kylie," he replied.

"I'll tell her you're here." She walked to the door behind her desk and after giving it a quick knock, she opened the door and announced Beau's arrival, then turned around and once again smiled at Beau. "She's ready for you."

"Thanks." He walked past Kylie and into Peyton's office.

As he'd noticed the day before, the room smelled

of her, a soft, feminine scent that instantly stirred his blood. He remembered that fragrance from the past… it smelled like sweet love and hot sex, like flowers and dark spices. For some reason it also prompted a touch of irritation in him because of the memories it stirred.

He tamped it down and smiled at her. "So where do we begin?"

"I've been trying to figure that out. I had Kylie send in a request for the official court files from the case. I should have them in hand in the next day or two. I also need to set up interviews with the Chief of Police who investigated the crime, and Charles Landry, who has since retired as prosecuting attorney."

As she talked, he couldn't help but notice how her blue blouse clung to the outline of her full breasts and matched the amazing color of her eyes.

His gaze took in the soft curve of her jaw and her sensual lips. Her dark, shiny hair was captured at the nape of her neck with a large gold barrette, and Beau's fingers itched to release the dark, silky tresses and allow them to spill through his fingertips.

His body responded, tightening against the crotch of his jeans. He hated himself for wanting her again and he hated her for abandoning him in his greatest time of need.

"Is Thomas Gravois still the Chief of Police?" he asked, trying to focus on the matter at hand.

"He is… Why?"

"He and Charles Landry are two of the most prejudiced people around," he replied in disgust.

She held his gaze and for just a moment he saw a softness there. But it was there only a moment and then gone as she looked back at her computer screen.

"In any case, I need to speak to them, and these are things I need to do alone. In fact, I can investigate the elements of the crime on my own and without any need for you to be with me." She looked back at him again, and this time her eyes held a steely strength.

Beau laughed. "Ah, Peyton, there is no way I intend to take a backseat in my own life. I've spent the last fifteen years alone and unable to do anything to help myself. We work together on this, and I know where we can start right now."

"Where's that?"

"At the Black Bayou Motel, room seven."

She sucked in a quick breath. "There's no reason to go there. It's been fifteen years since that room was rented by Lacy Dupree. There have probably been a hundred people who have rented that room since then."

He laughed once again. "That fleabag place hasn't seen a hundred renters since it first opened its doors fifty years ago." He sobered. "We need to start at the beginning, and the beginning happened in that motel room."

"I'm sure that room is probably rented right now," she protested.

"It's not. I stopped by there and checked before I

came here. Ed Johnson said he'd open up the room for us if we came by this afternoon."

"I just don't think that's necessary." Her reluctance was rife in her tone.

"But it is, Peyton," he said fervently. "I need to go back into that room and see if I can remember anything from that night that would prove I didn't kill Lacy. And I need you there with me so I can explain exactly what happened."

She searched his features as if seeking an out. But this was something he definitely wanted...*needed* to do with her and not all alone. Perhaps he was afraid that Lacy's spirit haunted the room—being Cajun, Beau had a healthy respect for spirits of all kinds.

"When do you want to do this?" she finally asked.

"Why not right now? I'm assuming you have nothing else on your calendar for today, so let's go." He stood. "We can get this step out of the way."

"Are you absolutely sure this is necessary?" Her eyes had darkened.

"Positive." He stepped around her desk and held his hand out to her. For a moment she looked at it like it was a snake that might bite her, but then she slid her hand into his and allowed him to pull her up from the chair.

Her hand was just as he remembered it, small and soft and a perfect fit in his grasp. He only got to enjoy it for a moment before she snatched it away from him. She bent down and grabbed her purse from beneath the chair and then stood back up. "I'm assuming I'm driving."

"Unless you want to walk," he replied. "My to-do list tomorrow includes getting a phone and finding a set of wheels." He'd intended to get a phone today, but he just hadn't taken the time to get it done.

Beau followed Peyton out of her office, where she told Kylie they'd be back later.

Together they walked out into the sultry heat of the afternoon. She led the way to a compact navy blue car and once she unlocked it, he slid into the passenger seat. Peyton got into the driver's seat and once again the scent of her swept over him.

He couldn't think about her and the surprising amount of desire she still evoked in him. He needed to be clearheaded to go back into the motel room where he supposedly had killed a woman. And it hadn't been just any woman; it had been one of his very best friends—although few had known that Lacy and Beau had a relationship of any kind.

The Black Bayou Motel was a dismal place. The low, flat-roofed building was weathered to a dull gray and reflected an air of hopelessness and despair. The people who stayed in the eight-unit motel were mostly drunks, drug addicts and prostitutes who rented the rooms out by the month.

Peyton parked in front of unit seven and Beau got out to walk to the office to get a key. He would never admit it to Peyton, but he was dreading going into that room, where he'd last seen Lacy alive and well. To know that she'd died such a horrible death mere minutes or hours after he'd left her there would forever haunt him.

He knew there were no clues to anything still inside the motel room, but he felt as if he needed to go in there to say a proper goodbye to another woman he had loved and lost, and he hadn't wanted to go in there alone.

Five minutes later he unlocked the door and the two of them walked inside. The room held a double bed covered in a nappy gold spread, a banged-up dresser and a small kitchenette. The air smelled musty and stale.

Beau stood in the middle of the room and closed his eyes for a moment. In his mind's eye he remembered the room the way it had looked when Lacy had lived in it.

She'd hung a variety of colorful scarves to hide the ugly gold curtains at the window, and her perfumes had littered the top of the dresser. Multicolored fairy lights had twinkled on the walls as she'd tried to make something beautiful in the room.

I'm sorry, Lacy, he thought. *I'm so sorry I wasn't here to protect you. If only I'd stayed longer with you that night, maybe then you wouldn't have been killed.*

"Beau?"

Peyton's voice ripped him back from the past.

His eyes snapped open. "Yeah," he replied.

She stood just inside the door and gazed at him curiously. "What are we doing here? Even if by some miracle you could find a piece of evidence to prove your innocence, it would do us no good because of a chain of custody issue."

"I knew we wouldn't find anything here," he replied.

She frowned. "Then why did you bring me here?"

"Ghosts," he said softly. "I needed to come here and I didn't want to come alone," he confessed. "I was afraid her ghost might be here to haunt me."

"There's no such thing as ghosts," Peyton replied, not unkindly.

"Maybe not in the ivory tower where you grew up, but we people from the swamps, we know there are ghosts and monsters and all kinds of darkness. In any case, I brought you here to tell you exactly what happened that night. I've waited fifteen years to tell you."

He couldn't keep away the edge of resentment that bit into his words. The early morning he'd been arrested, he'd been sure that she'd rush to the jail to speak to him, to profess her belief in him and remind him of her undying love for him. But she hadn't come then and she'd never come. And as much as he wanted her back in his bed, that resentment would always remain between them.

Chapter Three

Peyton waited for Beau to continue, even as all her defenses rose to the surface. She wanted to help him, if he truly was an innocent man, but did she really want to hear about his time here in this room with a prostitute? Still, a million times in her thoughts she'd wondered about the moments he'd spent with *her*.

Peyton had been a virgin when she'd slept with Beau for the first time. Maybe he'd needed somebody with more experience as a lover? Lacy would have definitely been a more experienced sexual partner than Peyton had been.

Maybe it was best she heard him out, no matter how painful it might be. She'd spent the past fifteen years wondering about that particular night. The truth was surely less painful than her imaginings.

"Lacy was a swamp kid like me," he said, leaning with his back against the wall next to the bed. "I was about seven and she was nine when we first met. Her dad and mine were drinking buddies and her mother had left them when she was seven. Even though she was a couple of years older than me, she always felt like my younger sister. I was her protector while we were growing up and being dragged along to boozing parties by our fathers."

"Why didn't I know anything about her?" Peyton asked. She'd thought she knew everything there was to know about Beau, and yet he'd never mentioned Lacy's name to her.

"Because Lacy wanted it that way." He raked a hand through his thick, shiny hair and released a deep sigh. "She made me promise that I wouldn't speak of her, that I would never tell anyone about our friendship. She knew that you were from an affluent family, and she also knew you had awakened big ambitions in me." He frowned and she saw a flash of pain in his eyes. He quickly broke eye contact with her.

"She thought she would somehow taint me, that people wouldn't take me seriously if they knew I was friends with a known prostitute."

He stood still for several long moments. However, even standing still he radiated an energy that seemed to pulse in the air around him.

He took several steps toward Peyton and his eyes blazed with a fire that nearly stole her breath away. He reached out and grabbed her hand, his grasp feeling fevered. She could also feel the furnace of his body heat and smell the scent of spicy cologne, the woodsy smell of mysterious swamp and utter maleness.

"Lacy and I were friends, Peyton. But we were

never lovers." His hand tightened around hers and the flame in his eyes intensified. "Do you hear me? We were never, ever lovers. That part of me always belonged to you."

"Beau, let go of me," she said and tugged her hand from his.

He immediately stepped back from her. She hated how his nearness still made her half-breathless. He was the only man she'd ever had in her life who affected her on such a visceral, physical level. "So why were you here that night?" she asked, focusing on what was really important.

"Lacy called me and said she needed to borrow a couple hundred bucks from me. She'd never asked to borrow money from me before, so I knew something must be up. So I showed up here that night to bring her the money."

"Did she tell you what she needed it for?" Peyton asked.

He shook his head. "She didn't, but she did tell me she was expecting a big payday and then she intended to disappear from Black Bayou. She also said the money from me would get her out of town in case things went sideways."

"A big payday? Did she tell you the specifics of what that meant?"

"No, she refused to tell me, but I got the feeling she was going to try to blackmail somebody, and I think that somebody is the person who killed her."

"But what about your necklace? Beau, it was around her neck when she was found."

"Don't you remember, Peyton? I'd lost my necklace about a week before her murder. You have to remember that. I was so upset about losing it."

Peyton stared at him. Suddenly, a memory formed in her head, the memory of Beau stalking across the floor of his bedroom, upset about the gold cross that had been lost. The cross had been the first thing he'd bought for himself when he'd worked his first carpentry job. Somehow, the memory had been buried beneath all the heartbreak she'd suffered when he'd been arrested.

"I... I do remember," she now whispered.

"She was alive when I left her that night. Somebody must have found my necklace and used it to kill Lacy and frame me for the murder." The words bit out of him with a simmering rage. "Dammit, somebody stole not only Lacy's life, but also fifteen years of mine, and more than anything I want the bastard in jail." He drew in a deep breath and released it slowly. "Now, let's get the hell out of here."

Minutes later they were on their way back to her office. Beau was silent, but his silence felt charged. Meanwhile, Peyton's head reeled with all the information she'd just learned.

Had he really told her the truth about that night? About his relationship with Lacy? It appalled her that she now remembered him losing his necklace at least a week before it was found as a murder weapon.

She now cast him a surreptitious glance. He stared out the front car window as a muscle knotted and un-knotted in his jaw. How difficult had it been for him to go back to that room? No matter what his true relationship had been with Lacy, that had been the place where a poor young woman had died a tragic death.

She pulled up in front of her office and the two of them got out. She'd told Kylie before they left that she could finish making calls on the accounts receivable and then she could take off for the day. She'd obviously finished up and left.

Beau followed Peyton into her office and they took their seats, she behind her desk and he in front of it. "So what happens next?" he asked.

His eyes lingered on her. Dark and enigmatic, there was something there that created a shiver that threatened to walk up her spine. It wasn't a shiver of apprehension; rather, it was of something dark and delicious.

She glanced at her computer screen and frowned. "In the morning I'll see if I can set up interviews with Thomas Gravois and Charles Landry and we'll go from there. I don't think there's anything else we can do today."

"We can have dinner together at the café," he said.

"Oh, I haven't been to the café in years," she replied. After Beau's arrest, she'd been unable to go into the place where she and Beau had often eaten together, a place where they had been so happy.

"Then I'm sure Marie would love to see you again.

She always had a soft spot for you. Come with me, Peyton. I'm not asking for anything but that you share a meal with me." A lazy grin of amusement curved his sensual lips. "Or perhaps you're afraid."

"Don't be ridiculous," she scoffed. "Why would I be afraid?"

He leaned forward in his chair. His gaze bored into hers, then traveled down the length of her throat and lingered for a moment on the thrust of her breasts. He then met her gaze once again. "Maybe you're afraid you'll want me again."

A new irritation rose up inside her. "Don't be ridiculous. That's the very last thing I'm afraid of," she replied curtly. "But I see prison didn't knock any of your conceit out of you." He merely laughed, which angered her even more.

"So are you up to the challenge?" he asked, a twinkle in the depths of his dark eyes.

She grabbed her purse and stood. "I'm a criminal defense attorney, Beau. I'm always up for a challenge," she said. "Let's go eat."

She heard his low chuckle as he followed her out of the building. Damn the man for his ability to get under her skin. Damn him for making her remember that it had been a long time since she'd made love with a man.

Minutes later the two of them walked into the busy café. The scents were heady…of frying onions and andouille sausage, of shrimp and burgers and all kinds of vegetables. The café itself had the requisite counter across the front, booths against both walls and a row of tables down the middle.

The walls were a pleasant yellow with hand-painted murals, one of cypress trees laced with Spanish moss and another of the main street of Black Bayou.

She suddenly became aware of all the diners staring at Beau as a charged silence filled the air. As Beau took her by her arm and led her down the aisle toward an empty booth in the very back, several voices filled the air.

Murderer.

Swamp scum.

Go back to the swamp that spawned you.

To Beau's credit, he appeared to ignore the hateful words that followed them as they headed for the empty booth. The only way she knew it bothered him at all was in the subtle increased pressure of his hand on her arm.

They reached the booth and he slid in with his back against the wall while she sat on the opposite side, facing him. His handsome features were taut and the muscle in his jaw tense. She had the ridiculous desire to reach out and take one of his hands into hers. She didn't, instead saying softly, "I'm sorry, Beau."

"Apparently, this will be my new normal until we clear my name," he replied.

At that moment Marie came into the dining room and beelined for their booth. "Hey, Marie. You gonna let that swamp-sucking killer eat in here?" an older man Peyton didn't know asked.

"He did his time, Wally, and his money is as good as yours," she replied. "Why don't you fill your mouth with my good food instead of filling it with such hateful nonsense?" She held the man's gaze until he finally looked down at his plate.

She then continued to their booth and when she got next to Peyton, she pulled her up and into a big hug. Peyton hugged the plump woman back and fought against unexpected tears.

When Peyton had been a teenager and dating Beau, Marie had been the loving mother Peyton hadn't had at home. It had been Marie who had answered questions Peyton had about life and about love. It had been Marie who had given her the loving support that Peyton's parents should have given her.

She and Beau had spent many happy hours at a small table in Marie's kitchen. There had been warmth and laughter and love there.

Once Marie released her, Peyton slid back into her seat. "Ah, Peyton, you've grown up to become such a beautiful woman." Marie smiled warmly. "Of course, I always knew you would. Why have you not come in to see me since you've been back here?"

"I've just been so busy establishing my practice here," Peyton replied. It was a lie. Marie nodded, her eyes filled with a crafty knowing in their dark depths. In truth, this place had held far too many memories for Peyton.

"When I heard you were here, I just wanted to come out and see you," Marie said. "Now that you're here, don't be a stranger in the future." She gave Peyton's shoulder a loving squeeze, then with a warm smile at Beau, Marie turned and headed back toward her kitchen.

Moments later they had ordered and then a few minutes after that their drinks and food had been delivered. Peyton took a sip of her iced tea and then leaned back against the leather booth. She was still trying to process everything he had told her in the motel room.

"What?" he asked as her gaze lingered on him.

"I'm trying to figure out, after all this time, how we prove your innocence. The evidence is all gone. You have no idea who Lacy might have intended to blackmail."

He leaned forward, bringing with him that scent of his that threatened to muddy her senses. "It had to have been somebody prominent in the town, somebody who had money and standing. You know the girls who worked at the motel were this town's dirty little secret. I imagine lots of the married men visited those girls under the cover of night."

Peyton didn't want to believe that, but she suspected it was probably true. After Lacy's murder, most of the girls who had been working in the motel rooms had scattered to the wind, but over the years others had taken their places.

She took a bite of her salad and chewed thoughtfully. "Was Lacy friends with any of the other women?

Did she ever mention having a best friend who she might have confided in?" she asked after swallowing.

"I think she was pretty friendly with Angel Marchant," Beau replied.

"Do you know if Angel was questioned at the time of the murder?" Angel had also been working and living in the motel when Lacy had been murdered.

"I don't have a clue," he replied.

"Do you know where Angel is now?"

"No, but if she's in the swamp, I can probably find her," he replied.

"We might need to talk to her. I'll know more after I speak to Chief Gravois some time tomorrow," she replied.

"We," he replied. "After *we* speak to him."

She nodded in agreement. For the next few minutes they ate in silence. Despite the fact that her head was filled with thoughts of what she needed to do and where they needed to go next, she was still acutely aware of Beau.

His energy radiated out to her. With each bite he took, his gaze lingered on her and had the effect of a physical touch. She had only had two other lovers since Beau and neither of them had made her feel as loved…as wanted as she'd once felt in Beau's arms. He'd taken her to sexual pleasures she'd never achieved with anyone else. She'd never felt that emotional connection, that depth of intimacy, with any other man since Beau.

However, none of those things mattered now. Remembering him losing his necklace before the murder had taken place had gone a long way toward her believing he was innocent. But she still wasn't sure she believed he hadn't been one of Lacy's lovers, and that alone would keep her from ever being in Beau's arms again.

By the time they left the café, twilight had fallen. "Do you want me to drop you off someplace?" she asked him once they were back in her car.

"You can just drive to your house and I'll leave from there," he replied.

She shot him a sharp glance. "How do you know where I live?"

He gave her that lazy grin that she found so damned attractive. "I make it my business to know the things that are important to me."

She drove to her house and pulled up in the driveway. They both got out of the car. "Nice place you have here," he said.

She looked at the light gray house with the darker gray shutters and deep maroon front door and then gazed back at him. "Thanks. I like it here. It suits me. So I guess I'll see you in the morning."

"I'll walk you to the door," he replied. She didn't want him to, but knew that a protest from her would only earn him mocking her.

As they walked to the front door, she pulled her house key from her purse. "I might be a little late in the morning," he said when they reached her door. "I need to buy a phone and see about getting a vehicle."

"Beau, you're not on any set timeline as far as I'm concerned." She unlocked her door and then turned back to face him. "We haven't really discussed you working on the building. Certainly, if you intend to follow through with it, then when it comes time to order any supplies, I'll pay for those. That's only fair."

He hesitated a moment, nodded and then took a step closer to her. He stood so close his scent surrounded her and infused her with its wicked wildness.

She stood still and he reached out and gently touched the strands of her hair that had escaped her barrette throughout the day. "I appreciate your help in this mess," he said softly.

Her heart began to beat a frantic rhythm. She knew she needed to turn around and escape into her house, yet she was frozen in place as his fingers slowly trailed down the side of her cheek and across the vulnerable hollow of her throat.

The touch of his fingers elicited a heat deep inside her. Oh, she remembered how easy it had always been to get lost in him, to forget everything but the fire of his touch.

As he leaned even closer to her, her brain finally worked enough so that she moved sideways and batted his hand away from her. He laughed.

"I'll see you tomorrow," she said firmly and opened her front door.

"Peyton."

She turned to look at him once again. His eyes glittered as they swept the length of her. His sensual lips curled into a confident smile. "Just so you know… I do intend to have you in my bed once again."

His words, spoken with such confidence, with such sensual appeal, completely irritated her.

"I'll help you clear your name, Beau…but I will never be in your bed again."

He laughed. "Never say never, *ma chérie*."

Whatever else he intended to say, she didn't stick around to hear him. She stalked into her house and slammed the door behind her.

She leaned against the door and tried to catch the breath she'd lost the moment he had touched her. She'd survived Beau once in her life and in some ways still suffered the consequences. She'd be a fool to allow him back into her life in any kind of a personal way…and she was definitely no fool.

WALKING BACK INTO the Black Bayou Police Department the next afternoon was one of the most difficult things Beau had ever done. The last time he had been here he'd been in handcuffs, confused by the serious charges against him and afraid for the first time in his adult life.

Now, despite the fact that he was free and Peyton was by his side, he still had the aftertaste of that residual fear in the back of his throat and it ticked him off.

Earlier that morning Peyton had set up this meeting with the chief of police, Thomas Gravois. Upon their arrival, the deputy at the front desk had ushered them down a long hallway and into a small conference room and then told them the chief would be with them shortly.

"Remember what I told you," Peyton now said softly to Beau. "I talk, you listen. Don't let him get under your skin. This is my playground, not yours."

"I can't wait to get you into my playground," he replied with a grin. It was much easier to flirt with her than acknowledge the racing emotions inside him.

"Beau, if you aren't going to take this all seriously, then why should I?" Her blue eyes pinned him in place.

He snapped the smile off his face. "Trust me. I'm taking this all very seriously." He'd barely got the words out of his mouth when Thomas Gravois walked into the room and sat at the table, across from Peyton and Beau.

The chief of police was a tall, lean man in good physical shape. He had to be in his midfifties by now. He sported a head full of graying dark hair and sharp blue eyes that radiated intelligence.

Beau knew the man had been dirt-poor before he married his wife, Yvette. Yvette was from a respectable, wealthy family...one of the families who held a strong prejudice against the people who lived in the swamp.

At the time of Beau's arrest, Thomas had been a young man with the fire of needing to prove himself burning in his eyes. "Well, well. Beau Boudreau, you finally got out," Thomas said. "I hope you learned some things in prison and now intend to be a law-abiding citizen in my town."

"I was a law-abiding citizen when you arrested me," Beau replied. He kept his tone calm and measured even though the minute the chief had walked into the room, a sense of wild injustice, of raw bitterness, had risen up inside him.

Thomas looked at Peyton. "You called this meeting and I don't have much time, so what's this all about?"

"I'd like to get a copy of your murder book in the Lacy Dupree case," Peyton said.

"Why? That case was closed years ago," Thomas replied in obvious surprise.

"I believe my client here was innocent when he was convicted of the murder," Peyton said.

Thomas stared at her for a long moment and then sat back in his chair and released a deep laugh. "Your client? Oh, this is rich," he finally said. "He got to you again. Peyton, your parents were embarrassed and heartbroken when you were running around town with Beau years ago and now here you are, at it again."

The mirth on Thomas's face suddenly transformed into a self-righteous anger and he slammed his hands down on the table. "I'll tell you right now, that was a clean investigation. We followed the evidence and all of it led directly to your client."

Beau's muscles bunched. He wanted to reach

across the table and punch the man in the face, not for the way he was speaking about Beau, but rather for the things he'd said to Peyton. However, he knew he had to stay calm for her. If he lost his temper now, he'd ruin everything.

"If you're so sure of your investigation then you shouldn't mind sharing the murder book with me," Peyton replied smoothly.

Beau had never seen Peyton in this capacity before. Clad in a crisp white blouse and a pair of black slacks, she looked cool and professional. She was self-confident and poised and he found this side of her sexy as hell.

Thomas released a deep sigh. "I'll have to have somebody dig it out of the records department," he said begrudgingly. "That file has been put away for a lot of years."

"I'd really appreciate it and I'd like to have it on my desk sometime tomorrow," Peyton said, her voice firm.

"I'll see what I can do. Are we done here? I've got another murder investigation to tend to," Thomas said.

"Another murder?" Peyton asked curiously. She hadn't heard about any other murders in town.

"Babette Pitre was murdered two nights ago. Her body was found in the alley between the post office and town hall. Her throat was ripped out and right now we're in the middle of that investigation."

"Do you have any clues?" Beau asked. He knew

the Pitre family and had vague memories of Babette as a little girl.

"Your folk seem to think it's the work of the Honey Island Swamp Monster," Thomas replied to Beau.

Your folk. That spoke volumes to Beau, and a wave of anger rose up inside him toward the man he believed had rushed to judgment in Lacy's murder case. Peyton apparently sensed his rising emotion, for she placed a steadying hand on his arm.

"Then we'll let you get back to your investigation," Peyton said. "But I still expect that murder book on my desk sometime tomorrow." She rose and Beau also got up from his chair. "We appreciate your time, Chief Gravois."

Minutes later they were back in Peyton's car and heading back to her office. "That jerk," Beau finally said, breaking the silence that had momentarily existed between them. "I thought you were going to ask him some questions about his investigation."

"I was, but I realized I can get everything I need to know about the investigation from his murder book. It will hold photographs of the crime scene and all interviews that were conducted and witness statements. It will also have the autopsy and forensic reports."

"Then I look forward to seeing that book," Beau replied. "Maybe someplace in those files will be the information to clear my name and point to the real killer."

"Speaking of killing, who or what is the Honey Island Swamp Monster?" she asked. "I've never heard of it before."

"That's because the creature isn't here around our swamps, but rather supposedly in the Honey Island area. According to the legend, the creature is an abandoned child raised by alligators. 'My folk,'" he said the words sarcastically and then continued, "the Cajuns, call the creature loup-garou, which means werewolf."

"So what does this so-called creature look like?" she asked with a curious glance at him.

"He's about seven feet tall and weighs around four hundred pounds. He's covered in dingy gray hair and has large, amber-colored eyes. He's three-toed and emits a horrendous stench. Now that I think about it, it's very possible Chief Gravois might be a direct descendant of the beast."

Peyton laughed. It was the first real burst of laughter he'd heard from her, and it reminded him of how often they had laughed together in the past. "You are so bad," she finally replied. "I suspect Babette was killed by a monster of the human variety."

"That would be my guess as well," he said.

She pulled up at the curb in front of her office and they got out of the car. They had only gone about three steps when her phone rang. She looked at the caller ID. "I need to take this really quick," she said to Beau. "You can go on inside and I'll catch up with you."

Before Beau could move away, he heard her answer her phone. "Hi, Sam." Her voice was low and pleasant and a swift, unexpected wave of jealousy punched through Beau.

He walked away, wondering who the hell Sam was. On an intelligent level he knew it was none of his business, but on a visceral, emotional level he wanted to know every man she had ever dated, every man who had been her lover since him.

He went into the building and Kylie jumped up from her desk. He motioned her back down with a smile. "Peyton's outside on the phone and will be in shortly. By the way, do you know who Sam is?"

"That would probably be Sam Landry," Kylie replied.

"And who is Sam Landry to Peyton?" he pressed.

"He's a nice man…a very respectable banker and uh…he and Peyton have been dating a little bit."

"Ah, good to know," Beau replied even as that niggle of jealousy swept through him again. "I'll just wait for her inside." He walked on through into her office and sank down in the chair facing the desk.

He'd had fifteen years to think about Peyton; fifteen years of wanting her again. Even though he'd felt betrayed by her and had been angry that she'd so easily believed him guilty of the murder, he'd counted down the days until he would see her again.

For him, life had stopped when he'd been arrested, but he now realized that, of course, life hadn't stopped for her. How serious was her relationship with this Sam?

How many other men had held her in their arms, tasted the sweet honey of her lips? How many other men had watched her eyes flash and darken with unbridled passion?

He sat up straighter in the chair as she came into the room and sat behind the desk. "Sorry about that," she said.

"Did the good, respectable banker ask you out for another date?" he asked, unable to help himself.

She froze and stared at him. Then she shook her head and released a small, dry laugh. "I see my trusty assistant has a big mouth."

"You didn't answer my question." He got up out of the chair and propped his hip on the edge of her desk.

Her cheeks flushed a soft pink. "It's really none of your business, Beau."

"Kylie said you've been dating the good Sam. Is it something serious?" His heart accelerated its beat. Her answer suddenly seemed exceedingly important to him.

"We've only gone out a couple of times," she replied.

"Have you slept with him yet?" he asked.

"Definitely none of your business," she replied sharply.

"I was just wondering if when he kisses you, do you moan in the back of your throat like you used to do with me? Does he know about that spot just behind your ear? The place where when I used to kiss you there, you'd writhe beneath me and moan my name?"

"Stop," she hissed angrily. "Stop it right now. And get off my desk." He laughed and returned to the chair. Peyton's blue eyes fired with anger, but in the very depths of them he saw something more…the sweet familiar flame of desire.

"You have to stop it, Beau. I can't work with you if you're trying to seduce me all the time."

"But you are so beautifully seducible," he said.

"I mean it, Beau. You have to stop. You're a client and as my client all I need from you is your honesty and your respect. Nothing more."

He sobered. "You have my utter respect, Peyton, and I will always be honest with you." Perhaps this was the way to her heart, instead of the seduction path he'd been on.

Then he wondered why he wanted to get into her heart in the first place. How could he ever love again the woman who, even for a moment, had believed he'd committed a heinous murder?

Chapter Four

Peyton leaned back in her chair and rubbed her tired eyes. A glance at the clock on the wall let her know it was after seven. She should have gone home several hours ago, but the murder book had finally arrived at her office at five, and since that time she had been completely engrossed in it.

She'd sent both Kylie and Beau home a couple of hours earlier. Thankfully, the murder book had arrived after they'd left the office. She found it difficult to concentrate when Beau was around. He was both a pain in her behind and a strange hitch in her heart.

Since he'd walked back into her life, she felt off center and overly emotional. He was forcing her to remember things she'd believed she'd shoved out of her head forever. He was making her feel that old breathless anticipation, the sweet flood of desire she used to feel for him. And she didn't want that. She didn't want him, she told herself over and over again.

She jumped at the sound of a knock on the building door. She got up from her desk and went into the reception area. Peeking out the window, she saw Jackson on the front stoop.

Quickly, she unlocked the door and ushered him inside. "Burning the midnight oil?" he asked.

"It's not exactly midnight, but I got caught up in something and lost track of the time." She ushered him into her office and he sat in the chair opposite her.

"Must be interesting for you to still be here at this time of night," he said. "A new case?"

"Actually, I've been reading the files from Chief Gravois on the Lacy Dupree murder case."

Jackson raised an eyebrow. "Any surprises?"

"A thousand." She sat back in her chair and frowned. "Chief Gravois insisted to me yesterday that it was a clean investigation, but it was practically no investigation at all. You know who the star witness was?"

"Who?"

"Louis Rivet," she replied.

"Really??" Jackson shook his head. "That man hasn't been sober for the last twenty-five years."

"Well, that was the prosecutor's star witness. He testified that Beau left the motel minutes after Lacy's time of death. He was innocent, Jackson. I believe Beau was really an innocent man when he was charged and convicted for the crime."

Jackson looked at her with surprise. "And you're sure about that?"

She thought about her conversation with Beau in the motel room and everything she had just read and seen in the murder book. "I'm positive," she replied.

"I think there was a rush to justice, and I suspect Beau probably had an incompetent lawyer, among other things. I'll know more about the counsel that represented him once I get the official trial documents."

"So if he really was innocent, then what happens next?"

"We need to find some new evidence that could overturn his conviction and get him a new trial," she replied.

"Whether he's innocent or not, I hope you aren't allowing him to get back into your head on a personal level." Jackson held her gaze.

"Trust me. I have it all under control." She would never admit to anyone how deeply Beau's touch still affected her, how his sensual smile still had the ability to weaken her knees and heat her blood. "So far we have a good working relationship and that's all it is."

"I've heard that the two of you have been seen around town. Gossip tongues are wagging."

She laughed. "Gossip tongues are always wagging in this town. I've never cared much what they are wagging about."

"A lot of people aren't very happy Beau has come back here."

"Where else would he go? This is his home," she replied.

"Have you heard from Sam since your last date?" Jackson asked, changing the subject.

"He called me yesterday."

"He's a good man. The two of you could make quite a power couple," Jackson observed.

"I do like him but we're taking things slow right now," she replied. "I intend to marry once and once only, so I don't want to make any mistakes. Now, what's going on in *your* love life?"

"I seem to be going through a bit of a dry spell," he said. "The women I ask out bore me. It's as if they're all cut out by the same cookie cutter. They're nice and sophisticated and absolutely boring."

"You've got to keep trying. You know you aren't getting any younger, Jackson."

"Don't remind me," he replied with a wince.

"You just have to find that special someone, Jackson. I know you'd be a wonderful husband and an amazing father."

"And you are only a year younger than me, and you aren't getting any younger, either," Jackson replied. "It's time for you to settle down, get married and have a couple of kids. Sam has told me he adores you. He'd make you a good husband."

"Duly noted," she replied.

"Well, I was just driving by and saw the lights on, but I was on the way to my parents' place for dinner." He stood. "Are you ready to leave? If so, I'll walk you out."

"Actually, I think I'll hang out here a little while longer. I want to finish up making some notes while things are still fresh in my mind," she replied. She got up as well. "But I'll walk you to the front door."

Minutes later Peyton was back at her desk, this time her thoughts filled with Sam Landry. Sam was a pleasantly handsome man. He was tall, with brown hair and hazel eyes. He had a kind face to match his kind personality.

She liked him and enjoyed his company, but so far there had been no real sparks with him. There was nothing even close to what she'd once felt for Beau. Of course, she'd been young and inexperienced when she'd first been with Beau.

But that doesn't explain how he still makes you feel, a little voice whispered inside her head. Memories… surely, that was all that was at play with Beau. She was no longer that young woman who had believed that he had hung the moon and stars.

Maybe she would never experience the feelings she'd once felt for Beau with any other man. Maybe she was a fool to even expect those kinds of fireworks again.

She returned her attention to making notes about what she'd read in the murder book. When she was finished, darkness had fallen outside. She stifled a yawn, locked up the files in her bottom desk drawer and then got ready to leave.

Tomorrow she would read through the files once again, looking for anything she missed the first time around. She also wanted to talk to Beau about seeing if he could find Lacy's friend Angel.

Maybe the woman would know something about who Lacy had intended to blackmail. Peyton believed that person was the real killer, and she would bet that person was still here in town. It ticked her off to know a murderer was still walking the streets freely and believing they'd gotten away with the horrendous crime.

She left the building and locked up. The night air was heavy and thick with heat and humidity. The sidewalks were deserted as she made her way to her car parked on the next block against the curb.

She reached her car and clicked the button on her key chain to unlock it. However, before she could even open the driver's door, she was shoved violently against it from behind.

A hard body held her in place against the hot metal of the car door as her brain worked to process what was happening. A burst of adrenaline filled her. She struggled in an attempt to get free, but he only shoved harder against her.

She knew it was a man. He breathed hard against the back of her neck. She could smell his sour perspiration and her heart beat frantically as fear raced through her. Who was doing this to her and why?

"W-what do you want?" she finally asked with a gasp. She prayed it was just a robbery and not anything else. "I have about a hundred dollars in cash in my purse. Let me go and I'll give it all to you."

"I don't want your damned money. Drop your investigation and let Lacy Dupree rest in peace." The voice was a deep growl that she didn't recognize. "Let sleeping dogs lie. This is a warning to you." He suddenly slammed his fist into the side of her face and then released her.

Pain seared through her cheek, dizzying all her senses. As she slumped against the side of the car, she heard his footsteps running away. She managed to get into the car and quickly locked the doors.

Dear God, what had just happened? She raised a hand to her cheek, the pain still throbbing with a breathless intensity. As the adrenaline that had momentarily filled her ebbed away, tears of residual fear and pain sprang to her eyes.

Who was that man? She should probably call the police and make a report, but she wouldn't be able to tell them anything about the man who had just assaulted her. All she knew for sure was that it had been a male.

It had all happened so fast. Even now she was having trouble processing what had just happened. She should have turned around to see him as he ran away. At least then she would have been able to give law enforcement a description of his general height and weight and maybe even a hair color. But she hadn't done that and so she saw no point in making a report.

She finally pulled herself together enough to start her car, even though she continued to cry. All she wanted to do now was go home and lock all her doors and windows. Despite her fear and her weeping, one thing was very clear: they had only just started the investigation, but they had already made somebody very nervous and angry.

Eventually, she pulled into her driveway and parked. As she got out of her car and made her way to her front door, she kept her gaze shooting all around, afraid that somebody might come out of the night shadows to attack her again.

She only breathed a sigh of relief once she was inside with the door locked. She headed directly to the kitchen, where she placed a few ice cubes into a towel and then held it up to her throbbing cheek.

She walked back into the living room and sank down on the sofa, still shaken by what had just happened to her. Had she just had an encounter with the man who had set Beau up? A shiver walked up her spine at the thought. Had Lacy Dupree's real killer just warned her off the case?

BEAU GRINNED AT the old man standing next to the rusty old black pickup truck in the large parking lot of Vincent's Grocery. The little store stood at the very edge of the swamp and was the place where a lot of the swamp people not only shopped but also parked their vehicles.

Gator Broussard was a legend in the swamps. Nobody knew exactly how old he was, but what Beau did know about the man was that he was a rascally character who had spent his life hunting gators. He was missing three fingers on his left hand, the result of a fight with one of the big beasts.

He was clad in a dingy gray T-shirt, and his worn jeans were tied around his thin waist with a rope. He carried with him a crooked walking cane that had a knife tied to the end.

Somehow, Gator had heard through the grapevine that Beau needed a vehicle and he'd gotten word to Beau to meet him here. "How have you been, Gator?" Beau now asked.

Gator's dark eyes twinkled. "Can't complain. I reckon I've been better than you've been. How you doing, Beau?"

"I haven't exactly gotten a hero's welcome back here, but I'm getting by."

"You got a raw deal, boy. There's no question in my mind about that. I knew at the time you would never hurt Lacy, but a bunch of the powerful people in this damn town made you take the fall so they could sweep it all under the rug and protect one of their own." Gator punctuated his words by spitting a stream of tobacco juice onto the ground next to him.

"Thanks, Gator, I appreciate it."

Gator nodded, his white hair glittering in the early-morning sun. "Now, I heard you were looking for some wheels." He put his hand on the side of the truck. "This don't look like much, but it runs like a top. They took my license a couple of years ago after I plowed into a parked car and they made me take a test that I flunked. Anyway, it's yours if you want it. I ain't got any use of it anymore."

"I appreciate your offer, Gator, but I'll buy it from you." Beau didn't want to be beholden to anyone. Besides, he knew how hard money was to come by for many of the people who lived in the swamp.

"Okay, I'll take a hundred for it," Gator said.

"No way. I'll give you five for it," Beau replied.

"Two," Gator countered.

Beau laughed. "I'll give you four hundred and that's the end of it." He pulled out his wallet and counted the bills into Gator's good hand. Gator tucked the money into the front pocket of his saggy, worn jeans.

"What have you heard about Babette Pitre's murder?" Beau asked the old man curiously.

Gator's eyes darkened and his smile disappeared. "Nothing much. Just enough to know it's the same as the last two."

"The last two?"

"Colette Castille and Marcelle Savoie were also murdered." Gator spit another stream of tobacco juice.

"When was this?" Beau asked in stunned surprise.

Gator frowned, his wrinkles attempting to take over his entire face. "Colette was about four months ago and Marcelle was about four or five months before that."

"What does Gravois have to say about it?"

Gator's weathered features screwed up into a deeper frown. "He says as little as possible. That man couldn't find a killer in a maximum-sentence prison," he said in obvious disgust.

"Gravois told me *my folk* believe Babette's murder is the work of the Honey Island Swamp Monster," Beau said.

Gator gazed around with slightly widened eyes as if just speaking of the beast might conjure him up. He finally looked back at Beau. "I don't know what kind of a monster ripped the throat out of those women, but it was definitely a monster."

The two talked for a few minutes longer and then parted ways with Beau having the title and the keys to the pickup. Before meeting Gator, Beau had gone to the cell phone store. He now had a phone and a vehicle and it was past time he got to Peyton's office to get some work in. Eventually he'd need to get to the license bureau and see about getting a new driver's license.

He was pleased that the truck fired right up, and as he drove, he thought about what Gator had told him about the two previous murders. Apparently, somebody was viciously killing young women from the swamp, and it didn't sound like much of anything was being done about it.

Unfortunately, Beau was in no position to do anything about it himself. At the moment he had to stay focused on finding Lacy's killer. Gator had told him where to find Angel Marchant, and Beau was hoping that later today, he and Peyton could go speak to the woman who had been friendly with Lacy before her death. Maybe…just maybe the woman would have some information to help.

He parked down the block from Peyton's office and then walked the rest of the way. He still needed to do a lot of work on the front of the building in order to get it into good enough shape for a new paint job.

However, before he got to that work, he wanted to tell Peyton about Angel. "Hi, Beau," Kylie greeted him when he walked in, but she didn't quite meet his gaze.

"Is she free?" he asked.

"She is. You can go ahead in," Kylie replied.

He walked into the office and Peyton looked up from her computer and half-stood as he came into the room. As usual, she looked beautiful. She was clad in a gray pair of slacks and a purple blouse that perfectly matched the vivid bruise on her cheek, a bruise that instantly tightened all his chest muscles.

"What happened?" he asked as he sank down in the chair facing her.

"Nothing important." She reached up and touched the bruise. Her gaze shifted to the left of him, and he immediately knew she was lying.

"Why don't you tell me what happened and I'll decide if it's important or not," he replied tersely.

"I…uh…just had a bit of an encounter last night when I left here," she said, still not meeting his gaze.

"An encounter with what? A ticked-off boxing kangaroo?"

A small laugh escaped her, followed by a wince. "Please, don't make me laugh." She quickly sobered and released a deep sigh. "I was getting ready to get into my car last night when a man came up behind me and slammed me into the car door. Then he hit me and ran away."

Beau frowned at her as a rich anger punched him in the gut. "And who was this animal who hit you?"

"I don't know, Beau. I didn't see him at all."

"Did he say anything to you?" Beau worked it around in his head. Why would a person just randomly sneak up on her and punch her in the face? There had to be a reason for the assault.

She looked away. "He might have said a few things to me," she finally said, reluctantly.

Beau got out of his chair and walked over to stand close to her. "What did he say, *ma chérie*?" What he wanted to do more than anything was stroke his fingers over her bruised cheek in an effort to magically heal her. What he also wanted to do more than anything was find the person responsible for her dark bruise and do more than just punch him in the face.

She once again met his gaze and raised her chin. "He basically told me to drop the investigation and let Lacy rest in peace."

Beau cursed soundly. So she'd been hurt because of him. "That's it, then. You're officially off the case."

"No, Beau. Don't you see? We've only just begun our investigation and already we've made somebody very nervous," she replied.

"I will not put you in a position for anyone to hurt you again," he said angrily. "I'll take it from here and you're done."

"No, I will not be done," she protested, her eyes snapping with blue fire as her chin rose up another notch. She got up from her chair and stood to face him. "I'm a criminal defense attorney and this isn't my first rodeo. I've had plenty of death threats in my career and this only makes me want to work this case even harder."

He could stand it no longer. He took another step closer to her and reached out and gently touched her cheek. "I would kill a man for hurting you," he said softly.

She didn't reply, but her lips parted slightly as if in open invitation, and her eyes darkened in the way he remembered from long ago. Suddenly, he was thrown back in time, back to when she was his and their passion and love for one another was overpowering.

Before he knew his own intent, he leaned forward and captured her lips with his. Instantly, a fire lit in the depths of his very soul. He'd initially meant the kiss to somehow soothe and comfort her, but as she opened her mouth and returned the kiss, it became one to possess and consume.

Her soft, pillowy lips offered sweet, hot honey that he wanted to drink forever. Unfortunately, all too quickly she gasped and took a step back from him.

"Consider that a moment of weakness on my part," she said as she sank back down in her chair. "And trust me. It definitely won't happen again." Her chin rose again in a show of defiance.

The kiss had shaken him up more than he wanted

to admit, and he could swear he saw a hint of desire still in the depths of her eyes. However, he couldn't allow what had just happened to deter him from the conversation they'd been having beforehand.

"What's important here is that you stay safe, and the only way that will happen is if you completely distance yourself from me and the investigation," he said.

"And I refuse to do that," she replied. "I'll just be smarter from now on with my personal safety. I'm moving forward with the investigation, and you can either be a part of it with me or not."

There was that strong, tough woman that he found so appealing. He'd known her as a young girl and now it was magnificent to see the woman she had become.

"Then I will be at your house and follow you to work each morning, and then I will see you home safely each night," he finally said. "I will be your bodyguard and nobody will ever get close enough to you to hurt you again."

"And how are you going to accomplish that?" she asked.

"As of this morning I am the proud owner of a pickup truck, so I now have the wheels to follow you back and forth each day, or better yet, drive you to and from the office and home."

She held his gaze for a long moment and then slowly nodded. "Okay, I'd appreciate that."

Her reply let him know that she'd been shaken up

by the attack more than she'd initially let on. The hot burn of anger once again licked his insides. He sat in the chair facing her. "Did you call Gravois and make a report of the attack?"

"No, I didn't bother. I didn't see the person who hit me so I couldn't give any identifying information to Gravois."

"I don't know what that man does all day, but he should be working overtime." He told her what Gator had said about the other two murders.

"That's terrible. I've kind of been following it on the news, although there hasn't been much talk about the murders in town. I certainly hope the killer is caught soon," she replied. "But we have to stay focused on Lacy's murder."

"Speaking of that, Gator also told me where to find Angel. She's deep in the swamp and has become something of a recluse. But he told me the general area where to find her, so I thought we could do that later this afternoon."

"Good. Maybe she'll have some answers for us," she said with a touch of excitement in her voice.

He got up from his chair. "I'll just head outside now and get some work done and then I'll be back in later this afternoon."

"I'll see you later," she agreed and immediately cast her gaze back at the computer screen.

Minutes later Beau was outside the office and working. As he worked, he thought about the attack on Peyton. Even though there was a core inside him that was still angry with her for not believing him years ago, the idea of anyone putting hands on her made him see red.

This afternoon they would venture into the swamp together, a place they hadn't been together in years, and he couldn't help but wonder what kind of emotions that might evoke in both of them.

Chapter Five

Peyton released a deep sigh once Beau left her office. She'd been foolish to think she could keep the details of the attack on her from Beau. She'd never been able to lie or keep secrets from him in the past.

She'd tossed and turned all night long thinking about the investigation, but not once had it entered her mind to quit. Somewhere out there was the real killer of Lacy, and whoever it was, the investigation had made him nervous enough to attack Peyton and warn her and Beau off.

There was no question she felt safer knowing Beau intended to get her home safely each evening. There was also no question that the attack had shaken her. But she wasn't giving up. The one thing the assault had done for her was positively clear any lingering doubt she'd had about Beau's guilt.

Beau…he was a complicated puzzle in her brain. His touch still had the ability to stoke a fire inside her and take her back to the simpler time when he was the love of her life.

On the surface he still appeared to be the slightly irreverent, slightly cocky man he'd been when he was twenty-one. Despite spending almost a week with him she still felt as if she hadn't really seen the real man he had become.

He had spent fifteen years in prison. That had to change a person at their very core. It had to have changed Beau in ways she couldn't even begin to imagine. And she wondered why she cared. She was just doing a job with him and that was it. Wasn't it?

Even though she now believed he was innocent of the crime against Lacy, she couldn't go back to that place and time when she'd been a young, innocent girl and he'd owned her heart so completely. Still, as her first lover, he would always have a special place in her heart, she supposed.

She shoved these thoughts aside and pulled up the official trial record from the Lacy Dupree murder case. They had been emailed to her that morning from the county records department and she was eager to read through them and see just how badly Beau had been represented by his public defender.

At noon Kylie brought her a sandwich and she ate as she continued to read and take notes. Beau had left, presumably to shower up and return after working through the heat of the morning.

It was almost two when she was interrupted by Kylie knocking on the door. "Mr. and Mrs. Farineau are here to see you."

Peyton looked at her in surprise. "Did they say why?"

"No clue," Kylie replied. "They wouldn't say."

"Then send them in."

Jason Farineau was part of the old guard in town. He'd made a fortune in investments and was on the city council. He entered the room like an angry bull, with his timid wife, Irene, trailing after him.

Peyton rose from her chair and shook both their hands. "Whoa, who whooped you in the face?" Jason asked.

Peyton raised a hand to her cheek. "I…uh…hit it on a cabinet door. Now, what can I do for you?" she asked once they were all seated.

Irene immediately pulled a tissue from her purse and began to dab at tear-filled eyes. Jason shot her a look of utter disgust and then looked back at Peyton.

"Yesterday my dear wife was caught shoplifting from Chastain's." His voice held a simmering anger. Chastain's was a high-end shop that sold both clothes and decorative items.

"Obviously, she wasn't thinking straight and this is all a big mistake. She had a damned credit card in her purse to pay for the items, but Chastain is pushing Trevor Mignot to throw the book at her and charge her with felony theft, among other things." Trevor Mignot was the current district attorney.

Jason leaned forward, his nostrils flaring. "I need you to make this all go away."

"I'm going to need a lot more information," Peyton replied and turned her attention to Irene. The woman looked positively terrified, and Peyton wasn't sure if she was more afraid of the charges against her and the possibility of a trial or her husband's wrath.

If the store was pushing for a felony charge, then that meant Irene had taken at least fifteen hundred dollars' worth of merchandise. Still, at the pricey store it wouldn't take too many items to reach that dollar amount.

"I just got confused," she said, tears slowly sliding down her cheeks. "I would never steal on purpose. It was just a big mistake and an accident." She glanced over to her husband and her tears came faster.

The meeting with the couple took approximately two hours. By the time they finally left, Peyton had agreed to represent Irene. When she walked them to the outside door she noticed that a thick layer of gray clouds had moved in, darkening the day with the portent of rain.

She turned back to Kylie and smiled. "I will be representing Irene on a shoplifting charge."

"Shoplifting?" Kylie looked at her in stunned surprise.

"Yeah, needless to say, don't mention this to anyone. She deserves her privacy and Jason just wants it all to go away. And speaking of it all going away, have you seen Beau?"

"Yes, he stopped in when you were with the Farineaus. He ran down to Larry's and said he'd meet you back here."

"Then I guess I'll get to work on the new case until he shows up here," Peyton replied.

"New case... I like the way that sounds, and the Farineaus should be able to pay cold, hard cash for your amazing defense skills," Kylie replied. "No payment plans for them."

Before either of them could say anything more, Beau came in. As always, he seemed to bring with him a simmering energy and a bold masculinity that somehow tapped into something deep inside Peyton. Damn him for still having the power to move her; damn him for still having the power to make her want him.

"I saw the Farineaus leaving here. New case?" he asked.

She nodded. "But it's nothing that will take up too much of my time." She turned to Kylie. "Get me a copy of the police report concerning the former matter."

"Will do," Kylie replied.

Peyton turned back to Beau. "Now, let's go find Angel and see if she has some answers for us."

"I'll drive," he replied.

She raised an eyebrow. "Do you even remember how to drive?"

"Of course I do. I've got my new set of wheels and I now have a cell phone. We can exchange numbers once we get to Vincent's parking lot."

"Let me just grab my purse," she replied.

Within minutes she was in the passenger seat of

his truck. On the outside, the truck was rusted and a bit banged up, but the inside was clean as a whistle and already smelled like Beau.

The closer they got to the swamp, the bigger a ball of anxiety pressed against her chest. She hadn't been back in the swamp since the last time she'd made love with Beau, when she'd still believed in a bright and wonderful future with him. Then the next morning he'd been arrested and her entire world had crashed down around her.

At that time he'd not only been her lover, but he'd also been her very best friend. She'd shared with him all her hopes and dreams and all her fears and disappointments. She'd believed him to be her soul mate. She now cast him a surreptitious glance and then quickly stared back out the front window.

It was still there. The powerful force that had once brought them together as friends and lovers years ago, it was still there…simmering just beneath the surface with intensity and volatility.

She didn't want it to be there. She could pretend that it didn't exist; she could even lie to Beau about it, but she couldn't fool herself. She was still hopelessly attracted to him.

He parked the truck in the big parking lot behind Vincent's Grocery. The small store mostly served the people who lived in the swamp. It was walking distance from the gravel parking to the mouth of several trails that entered into the dark marshland.

They got out of the truck and took a moment to

put their phone numbers into each other's phone and then they began to walk up a familiar trail.

As they continued to walk deeper into the tangled growth, what little sunlight there had been nearly disappeared, unable to filter through the trees and brush that surrounded them.

Insects buzzed around them and whirred a cacophony of sound, and from someplace nearby a fish or a gator slapped the water. Other small animals ran through the brush ahead of them, and Peyton made sure she stayed as close to Beau as possible.

He moved through the tangled underbrush with complete confidence, like a sleek wild animal in his own environment. At the moment they were on the path that would eventually lead them to his home, but before they reached it, he veered off on another narrow trail.

"Have you ever been to Angel's place before?" she asked.

"No—when I knew her, her home was in the motel next door to Lacy's room."

"Do you know where we're going?" she asked nervously.

He glanced back and flashed her a smile, his straight white teeth visible despite the lack of any real light. "Not exactly. Let's just hope the directions Gator gave me are good ones."

"Let's hope," she replied faintly.

It became darker, cooler, as they entered the heart of the swamp. Peyton's steps faltered and she slowed as the terrain grew more difficult to maneuver. Beau turned and offered her his hand. Eagerly, she grasped his, grateful for the warmth and strength as they continued on.

Birds cried discordantly from the tops of the trees, as if to protest the human trespassers. The air smelled both of strange flowers and more than a hint of decay. Fear, along with a healthy respect for the surroundings, filled her.

"How much farther is it?" she whispered, afraid of what she might awaken if she spoke too loudly.

"I'm not sure, but it shouldn't be too far now," he replied. "Gator gave me the directions to find it. Do you need to stop and take a rest for a minute or two?"

"No, I'm okay." And she was, as long as his hand continued to hold hers. It reminded her of how they had first met, when she'd been a kid lost in the swamp and he had been the hero who had gotten her safely home. There were times when she believed it had been on that night, at that tender age, when she'd fallen in love with Beau.

A howl filled the air, the chilling sound causing her heart to nearly jump out of her chest. "What was that?" she asked nervously.

"I'm not sure. It sounded like a wolf."

At that moment Beau stopped and pointed ahead to where a small shack stood on stilts. Several kerosene lanterns hung on the small porch area, illuminating a dozen or so macabre dolls that hung from the rafters.

"Wh…what are those?" she asked.

"I don't know," Beau admitted. "But there's one thing I forgot to mention about Angel. According to Gator she's not only a healer, but she's also a witch."

A new icy chill suddenly walked up Peyton's spine.

THE WOLF HOWLED AGAIN and the door to the shack opened. Silhouetted in the light from within was a tall woman who held a rifle in her hands. "Who's there?" she called out.

"Angel, it's Beau. Beau Boudreau and Peyton La-Croix. We'd like to talk to you."

She didn't reply for several long moments. Beau hadn't realized just how much he'd hoped that Lacy had confided in Angel before her death until now, when he wasn't even sure Angel would agree to speak with them.

"Then come in," she finally replied.

As he and Peyton got closer to the shack, he saw that Angel had moved one hand from her rifle to the back of the large red wolf that stood beside her.

Beau's hand felt nearly strangled as Peyton tightened her grip on his. Her fear was palpable, and he had to admit a bit of disquiet raced through him as old legends of monsters and beasts and witches of the swamp filled his head.

They moved forward toward a small bridge that would carry them across the swamp waters and to her porch. Beau led the way, with Peyton nearly walking on the backs of his heels.

Angel disappeared from the doorway. The dolls that hung all around the porch were made of cloth with yarn hair and macabre features. Some had pins thrust into their bodies and faces while others had small knives protruding from their hearts. Were they representative of the people Angel had cursed?

He had no idea if Angel believed he'd killed Lacy or not, but he supposed he was about to find out. They walked into the shack to where Angel now sat in a large, dark brown chair, the wolf on alert by her side.

She gestured to the sofa that faced her chair and Beau and Peyton sat. "Beau Boudreau… I didn't expect to ever see you again."

"I didn't expect to ever see you again, either," he replied. "But fate has brought us together once again."

The last time he'd seen Angel she had been an attractive young woman with long black hair and dark eyes that had held a passion for life.

It had been fifteen years since he'd seen her, and he now wouldn't have been able to pick her out of a crowd. Her dark hair now held a white streak down the middle, and she looked as if she'd aged thirty years or more.

A ropey scar slashed across one of her cheeks, and her eyes now held a combination of what appeared to be weariness and a depth of wisdom.

He looked around the room. A variety of plants hung from the ceiling rafters; some he recognized and some he didn't. The air smelled of flowers and berries, of mysterious concoctions and spices. More dolls also hung in here.

"What's the deal with the dolls?" he asked.

She cast him a sly smile. "Haven't you heard, Beau? I'm the wicked witch of the swamp. Men fear me and women sneak here in the dark to see me for a variety of health issues and other things."

"You didn't answer me about the dolls," he replied.

"Beau, I'm a woman living alone here—other than my faithful companion, Wolf." The animal turned his head to gaze at her adoringly. "Making sure everyone sees me as a powerful witch or a voo-doo queen who makes dolls and curses people keeps most folk away from me, and that's the way I like it." She reached up and touched the scar on her cheek.

"As long as people are afraid of me, I am safe here." She touched the back of the wolf once again. She spoke in a language Beau didn't recognize. The wolf responded by lying down with his head on his front paws, but the yellow eyes continued to shoot between Beau and Peyton.

"I would think your friend there would keep most people away," Peyton said with a nod toward the wolf. "Where did you get him?"

"I found him as a newborn pup hidden in a thick bush. I found the bodies of his mother and father some ten feet away. They had been shot." Her eyes flashed darkly. "Damn hunters. Anyway, I brought him back here and I am now his mother and his fa-ther and his sister and brother. He would kill for me and I would kill for him. Now, why are the two of you here? It's been many years since I've seen either one of you."

Beau leaned forward in his seat. "First, I'd like to ask you a question. Do you believe I killed Lacy?"

A smile curled her lips. "Trust me. If I believed you murdered my friend, then you wouldn't now be sitting in my home. I know you didn't kill her."

"I'm now trying to figure out who *did* kill her," Beau replied. "Somebody murdered her and framed me, Angel. I want to know who that was, and we were hoping you might somehow be able to help us with that."

"I tried to tell Gravois at the time that you would never harm her, but he didn't even want to talk to me. I knew then that he wasn't really looking for the truth. One swamp person was dead and he got another one thrown in prison. That's all he was interested in."

"I visited her on the night of her murder. She needed to borrow some money from me," Beau said. "I got the impression she had plans to blackmail one of her...uh...clients."

Angel nodded. "She told me, and I told her that the plan would get her killed, but she wouldn't listen to me."

A flutter of hope swept through him. Had Angel known the answer all these years and just couldn't find anyone in local law enforcement to listen to her? "Did she tell you who he was?"

"Did she tell me his name? No. All she told me

was that he had money and was in a position in town where he would not want people to know he visited a prostitute on a regular basis."

The hope Beau had felt moments ago left him on a deep sigh. "So you don't have any information that can help us find out who he is."

"I can't give you a name, but I might have something here that will help you." As she stood from her chair, Wolf immediately got to his feet. She spoke a couple of words Beau didn't understand and the wolf sank down once again.

Beau watched as she walked over to one of the hanging dolls, one with wide eyes and a mouth that appeared to be screaming. She yanked it down and then walked over to a small desk just inside the front door and grabbed a pair of scissors. Beau shot a quick glance at Peyton, who appeared anxious, yet obviously curious.

"I'm not sure why I kept this for all these years," Angel said as she used the scissors to cut off the doll's head. She returned to her chair and began to pull out the stuffing. Along with the stuffing, a folded piece of paper fell out.

"I knew Lacy kept some sort of a list of her clients and that she hid it in a heat vent in her room, so a few days after her murder I went in and got it." She unfolded the piece of paper that was now a bit yellowed and frayed with age and then handed it to Beau. "I was afraid if I gave it to Gravois, he would just throw it away. I never knew who to give it to, so I just kept it."

Beau stared down at the paper, which held nothing more than a list of initials and numbers. He looked back at Angel. "These initials are for the men who visited her?"

"Yes," Angel replied.

"Do you think the killer's initials are here?"

"I'm positive of it," Angel said firmly.

"Do you have any idea what the numbers mean?" He asked.

"I don't," she replied.

"Why did you keep this for so long?" he asked her curiously.

"Maybe I held on to it all this time because on some strange level I knew one day you would need it to set justice right." Her eyes flashed darkly once again. "If I was truly a powerful voodoo queen, I would make sure Gravois suffered an accident that would cause him to suffer every day for the rest of his life as he has made so many of us suffer."

Once again, a wave of hope swept through Beau as he held the piece of paper tightly in his fingers. "Thank you for keeping this, Angel. It might help us solve Lacy's murder and let me reclaim my life as an innocent man," Beau said.

"And you are helping him with this?" she asked Peyton.

"I am," Peyton replied.

Angel smiled. "I heard what you did for the Mouton family. It was very kind of you."

"I just did what was right," Peyton replied.

Beau stood and Peyton followed suit. "Well, we'll just get out of here," he said. "Thank you, Angel... both for speaking with us and for potentially handing me the key to finding the killer." Angel remained seated and Beau paused at the door. "If I may ask... who scarred your face?"

Her hand reached up and touched the thick puckered scar. "Needless to say, Lacy's murder shook us all up, but we ladies of the night kept working. But it was as if there was a free-for-all in hurting us. Suzette had her arm broken, and about a week after that a client of mine didn't like something I said to him and he pulled a knife and slashed me."

She dropped her hand back to her side. "The next morning, I left the motel and found this place, which had been abandoned years before. I claimed it as my own and began to study herbal healing from the plants and flowers that are abundant around here." She raised her chin as pride shone from her eyes. "I like helping people with my herbal knowledge and now I have the power to pick and choose who comes into my life, and no man will ever get close enough to hurt me again."

"Are you happy here?" he asked.

"Happy?" She cocked her head and frowned thoughtfully. "I'm not sure, but what I do know is that I'm finally at peace. I'm content here with Wolf and the people I serve here in the swamp. Back then, when I was working out of the motel, I wanted to get up enough money to leave the swamp forever, but now I embrace the swamp, which has truly become my mother and my father, and I am no longer ashamed of who I am."

"I'm glad you've found some peace here, Angel," Peyton said.

Angel nodded and stood. Wolf immediately got to his feet next to her. "Please don't tell anyone you spoke to me and don't tell anyone where you found me. I can't do anything more for you than I already have."

"Again, we appreciate whatever force made you keep that piece of paper," Peyton said.

"I hope you find the killer who destroyed so many lives," Angel replied. A sly smile once again curved her lips. "I will make a special doll just for him and bring a thousand curses on his head."

Beau's blood chilled. Somehow, he believed she would do just that, and he was only grateful he wasn't the man she would curse.

Chapter Six

It was raining when Peyton and Beau left Angel's place. Peyton was eager to check out the piece of paper that Angel had provided to them, but at that moment she was too busy fighting against the torrential rainfall. Within several minutes she was soaked to the skin, but grateful that the rain was warm rather than cold.

Beau held her hand again as they traveled slowly through the unfamiliar terrain. It was inky dark, but thankfully, he had a penlight in his pocket. Even though the small light didn't help them look too far ahead, at least it lit the ground enough for them to know where to step without falling into the swamp waters.

"We'll go to my place and wait out the storm," he said, yelling to be heard above the sound of the rain beating against the leaves overhead and the thick brush.

Peyton nodded. Hopefully, the rain wouldn't fall for too long. Flooding in the swamps was always a danger. When they reached the place where they had to take the right trail to go to Beau's cabin, she had a moment of trepidation. The last time she had been in the cozy four-room shack, she and Beau had made sweet, passionate love.

She shoved her disquiet away. Nothing like what had happened years before between them was going to happen now. They would just wait out the rain and if it didn't stop in the next thirty minutes or so, she'd insist that he lead her on out of the swamp.

About twenty minutes later it was a welcomed relief to step into his front door. Here, it was as if time had stood still. Nothing had really changed since the last time she'd been here.

She walked over to the chair and sank down while he moved to the potbellied stove and began to build a fire. "Hopefully, a nice fire will help to dry us out a bit," he said. "Let me get this started and then I'll hand you a towel."

By the time the fire roared in the stove, Peyton had towel-dried her hair and clothing as best as she could.

"Do you want something to drink? I've got cold water and some soda." Beau walked over to a medium-size wooden box in the kitchen area.

"What is that?" she asked curiously.

"It's my home-made refrigerator. As long as I get bags of ice for it every couple of days, it keeps my meat and other supplies cold. If I somehow forget to buy the ice, I can plug it into my generator for just a little while." He opened the hinged top. "So what will it be?"

"I wouldn't mind a water," she said. He pulled out two bottles of water and then placed the lid back into place on the wooden box.

He handed her a water and then he sank down on the sofa while she remained seated in the chair facing him. They both twisted off their bottle tops and took several drinks of the refreshing water.

"Now I'm ready to see the paper that Angel gave you," she said as she put the lid back on the water bottle.

"Then come and sit next to me." He patted the space next to him on the sofa, set his water on the coffee table and then pulled the piece of paper out of his leather wallet. She got up and moved to sit next to him as he opened up the piece of paper.

Instantly, several things flashed through her brain. The scent of him, so wild and evocative, filled her head. His body heat seemed to reach out and fully embrace her.

She'd made love to him when they'd been so young. What would it be like to make love to him now? She was a far more confident, experienced woman than she had been then. She shoved those dangerous thoughts out of her head as she took the piece of paper from him.

She stared down at the string of initials that lined one side of the page with numbers written beside them. She'd hoped for something more. "I wonder what the numbers mean," she said.

"How many times the particular man visited her? Or perhaps some sort of rating system? We'll probably never know for sure what those numbers mean," he replied.

"Maybe they had something to do with how blackmail-vulnerable the men were."

"Perhaps," he agreed.

"So it looks like what we need to do is set up a spreadsheet and try to match up initials with the men in town." It was going to be a daunting task. "Then once we have the names, we'll have to figure out who Lacy's target was and that's probably our killer." She handed him back the piece of paper.

It was going to be a tough job. There were about seventeen sets of initials that needed to be matched up with seventeen men. It was certainly not going to happen overnight.

"Maybe I can get a list of the names of all the homeowners by going to the property tax records, but that won't give us the name of any renters in town, especially not from fifteen years ago," she said.

"I can't imagine Lacy blackmailing somebody who didn't own property or have their own house. Why don't you keep this until tomorrow?" He returned the paper to her.

She pulled her cell phone out of her pocket. "The first thing I'm going to do is take a picture of this." She aimed and then took two photos of the list. "The next thing I'll do in the morning is make a couple of copies of this," she said as she refolded the paper and put it into the bottom of her purse. "I also want to talk to Louis Rivet. Even though the man is an alcoholic, it was his statement that put you in the motel room minutes before Lacy died, and now knowing her time of death and what you've told me about that night, there is a huge time discrepancy."

"Do you really think he's going to remember something like that now?" Beau raised a dark brow in skepticism.

"Yes…no… I really don't know. I'm just hoping he saw somebody else go into Lacy's room after you left that night. I'll tell you what's really criminal… the fact that your defense attorney didn't even try to punch holes in Louis's memory and didn't bring up that Louis was totally pickled on most nights. I could probably argue to a judge that you had ineffective counsel and get you a new trial."

He frowned. "I don't want to win that way. I want to win by finding the guilty bastard who murdered Lacy and then framed me to take the fall."

"You realize that might not happen," she said softly.

"It *will* happen, because I won't stop until I have the answers. Now, tell me what you did for the Mouton family."

She blinked at the quick change of topic. "Oh, it was nothing really. Their youngest son had been caught spray-painting a building that Lester Granger owns."

"That old coot? I'm surprised that he's still alive," Beau replied.

"He's not only still alive, but he's also the cranki-est old man in town. He wanted to throw the book at the boy but I managed to get him off with probation and some community service. I also cut my fee in half and set them up on a payment plan. I would have done it for free, but I didn't want to hurt their pride."

"That was very kind of you, and you're right in that they would have been highly offended if you'd offered your services for free. That's one thing that can be said about swamp people—we have a lot of pride and they always try to pay their own way."

He turned and stared into the fire. For a moment he appeared haunted. His features were all taut lines and angles, and his eyes were as dark as the devil's heart.·

The rain had stopped and the swamp around them had come alive with bellowing frogs and insects that sang their nighttime lullabies.

"You must have missed this place when you were away," Peyton finally said, breaking the silence that had grown between them.

"You have no idea." He turned back to face her. "I grieved for the sound of the swamp…for the smells and the freedom of home."

"How did you survive? I mean, we've all heard horror stories of the vicious gangs and a variety of groups that provide protection to inmates in prison."

A slow grin curved his lips. "I didn't need a group

or a gang affiliation to keep me safe. Somehow, a rumor began that I was a voodoo priest and I lived in the deepest, darkest heart of the swamp with wild animals who did my bidding. In that respect Angel and I have a lot in common. Anyway, the other inmates believed I could cast powerful spells and curses and so for the most part they all left me alone."

He could definitely cast spells. Each time he smiled like that, every time he gazed at her the way he was doing right now, she felt as if he'd placed her in a dizzying spell of desire.

He reached out and unfastened the barrette she had on the nape of her neck. Her hair spilled into his fingers. "It will dry much quicker this way," he murmured.

She wanted to tell him to stop running his fingers through her hair. She needed to demand that he lean back from her and give her some space.

However, as his fingers trailed slowly down the side of her jaw and then across her mouth, she was frozen in place by his sensual onslaught. She fought for control despite her body responding to him.

"Stop it, Beau," she finally managed to gasp as she batted his hand away. "If you want to catch a killer then you have to stay serious."

His eyes glittered wickedly. "Right now I am very serious about seducing you."

"Well, it's not working, so give it up," she snapped. She grabbed her barrette from his hand. "It sounds like the rain has stopped and now I need to get home."

He laughed that knowing, confident laugh of a man who knew what his touch did to her, a man who enjoyed making her heart beat erratically.

When they left the shanty, she waited for him to go before her as she'd been away long enough that even this part of the swamp wasn't as familiar as it had once been, especially in the dark after a rainstorm.

He reached back and took hold of her hand and for just a moment she was cast back in time, to the first time she'd met him when he'd led her out of the swamp. He'd been her hero in that moment, and for years that followed before fate had stepped in to separate them.

She'd thought she could just help him in his endeavor to clear his name, but the truth of the matter was she was precariously close to being in love with Beau all over again. And she didn't like it. She didn't like it at all.

She understood now that he was not only innocent of murdering Lacy, but he also hadn't betrayed her love on that fateful night. He'd told her that he and Lacy had never been lovers and after all this time he had no reason to lie about it. She'd spent the past fifteen years hating him for something he hadn't done.

However, she was terrified of loving him again. He'd spoken so briefly of his time in prison and yet she knew that time had to have changed him.

Right now there was no question that he desired her, but could he ever love her again, and did she really want him to? She shoved these thoughts aside.

It was possible she held the key to Lacy's murderer in her purse right now. That was all she needed to focus on. Find the killer and then see if the two of them belonged together or not.

PEYTON WAS SEATED at her desk the next morning despite it being Saturday when Jackson walked in. *"Mon dieu,"* he exclaimed and stopped in front of her desk. "That man has only been back in your life for less than a week and already you've been hurt. Did he do that to you?"

Peyton reached up and touched her cheek. She'd nearly forgotten that the bruise was there. "Of course Beau didn't do this to me. He would never, ever hit a woman," she said indignantly. "I…uh…just hit it on a cabinet door in the dark in the middle of the night."

He stared at her for several long moments and then sat in the chair in front of her. "So what else is new besides you bouncing around off furniture in the dark and working on a Saturday?"

Peyton dropped her hand and hoped the bruise hid her blush. She didn't like to lie to anyone, especially to Jackson. But she didn't want to tell him what had really happened concerning the bruise because she didn't want to hear him go on and on about it.

"I've got another case, which is always a good thing," she said.

"That's what you should be doing, building your business, instead of chasing around and trying to find a killer from fifteen years ago."

"I can multitask and do both," she replied and smiled. "You should know by now that I'm an over-achiever."

"You were an overachiever when you were younger because you were desperately trying to please your parents. Since nothing you did was ever going to please the two of them and they wrote you off and moved to New Orleans, you don't have to prove any-thing to anyone anymore."

Jackson knew how hard she'd worked, how des-perate she had been to gain acceptance and love from her parents. It had taken her years to recognize that she was never going to get what she wanted...what she *needed* from them. She'd made peace with the fact that the problem hadn't been her, but rather her cold, distant and society-loving parents.

"I'm not trying to please anyone but myself," she finally replied.

"You're certainly not pleasing anyone in town. There's been a lot of talk about your investigation into Lacy's death. Nobody wants that can of worms reopened."

"Why? Why not open that can of worms? So no-body in this whole town cares about finding out the truth? Nobody cares that the real killer got away with his crime?" She looked at Jackson in disbelief. "You have always talked about the injustices and preju-dices that go on in this town against the swamp peo-ple. Why would you not want me to help a man who went to prison for fifteen years for a crime he didn't commit? How would anyone be okay with that?"

She paused to draw a quick breath and then continued. "Beau's only crime was that he was from the swamp and was easily disposable so Gravois could write *solved* on his résumé. I've seen the facts, Jackson. I believe in Beau's innocence with all my heart and soul, and I don't give a damn what the gossipers in this town think."

"He wasn't good enough for you then and he's not good enough for you now," Jackson said with a rise in his tone of voice.

She sat back in her chair and looked at him in surprise. "Jackson, I'm just helping him clear his name."

Jackson gave her a wry smile and shook his head. "I've known you for years, Peyton. I see the way your eyes light up when you mention his name. He's drawing you back in and I just don't want to see you get hurt by him again."

"Don't worry, Jackson. I don't intend to let him hurt me again," she assured him. "I'm much older and wiser this time around."

"Ah, but love can make a person feel young again. It can make a smart woman very foolish."

She laughed. "Oh, Jackson, you are such a cynic. Someday love is going to bite you in the butt and you'll become a foolish man."

"I don't see that happening. I'll probably eventually marry a woman to please my parents. That woman and I will enter into a relationship that financially and socially serves our best interests."

"And that makes me very sad for you," Peyton said to her friend.

Once Jackson left, their conversation played and replayed in Peyton's head. The two had often butted heads over the subject of love.

Jackson didn't believe the emotion existed, while she believed in a fairy-tale kind of love. She didn't want a business arrangement for a marriage; she wanted love to include desire and passion and an overwhelming sense of safety and belonging.

She spent the next couple of hours talking on the phone to the district attorney to see how strong the charges made against Irene Farineau were, and if there was any wiggle room at all to get the charges dropped as long as full restitution was made to the store.

Unfortunately, he couldn't give her an answer without speaking to Claude Chastain, the owner of the store. The DA promised to get back to her in the next couple of days.

Meanwhile, Irene had already been arraigned and released on her own recognizance. Peyton wished she would have been called to represent Irene at the arraignment, but that had taken place before the couple had reached out to Peyton. All she could do now was try to get the woman a lesser sentence, or best-case scenario, get the charges against her dropped altogether.

It was after one when Beau came into the office. He'd driven her there that morning and had been working on the building until noon, when he always disappeared and then returned smelling clean and clad in different clothes.

He had made her promise the night before that she wouldn't do anything with the note from Angel until he was with her. He hadn't even wanted her to look at it until he was present and they could work at it together.

"Good afternoon," he said as he grabbed the back of the guest chair, carried it around the desk and placed it next to hers. "I saw that Mr. Perfect stopped in to see you."

"Mr. Perfect? You mean Jackson? Why on earth would you call him Mr. Perfect?" She looked at Beau curiously.

"I always thought he'd make you the perfect husband. He's handsome and comes from the right social class. He has a trust fund and knows all the right people. And so, there is your perfect man."

She laughed. "There's only two problems with that—Jackson is a close friend and I'm not in love with him."

"In the last fifteen years, have you been in love?" His gaze held hers with a sudden intensity.

"That's really none of your business," she said. She reached for her purse and pulled out the folded note. "*This* is your business and the first thing I need to do with it is make a couple of physical copies."

She was aware of his gaze following her as she got up and walked to the copier machine in the corner of the room. "I'll give you a copy and I'll keep one for myself. The original I'll take to the bank and have locked into my safety deposit box." She brought the copies back to her desk and sank back down. "I think we should also give Gravois a copy of this."

"Why?" Beau asked, obviously not liking the idea of sharing anything with the chief of police.

"Because I'd rather work with law enforcement whenever we can. Besides, if nothing else, maybe his curiosity will help us solve this…this riddle we've been left with. Now, let's get started. We'll work on it for a couple of hours and then I need to run some errands."

"And I will go with you to run those errands," he said. She started to protest, but he held up a hand to stop her. "Your bruise has not even faded yet and already you've forgotten that you're in danger. I will go with you to run your errands."

"Okay, then let's get started on this puzzle of the initials." She opened up a spreadsheet on her computer. The first set of initials was GM. "Gustave Martin," he immediately said. "Does he still own half of the properties on Main Street?"

"He does, and he's married so he would make perfect blackmail material." As she typed his name into the spreadsheet, Beau leaned close to her. As always, his scent fired something deep in the pit of her. It was the wildness of the swamp coupled with a pure clean maleness that belonged to Beau alone.

He still had the ability to make her feel like that breathless teenage girl who had loved him more than anything else in the world. He still had the capacity to make her feel more emotions than any other man had in her life.

She mentally shook herself and focused on the initials. "There's also George Marcel. He's also married and has family money." She added his name into the computer. "We'll just go down the list and add the names that easily pop up in our heads. Then once I get the property tax records later this afternoon, we can add in anyone we missed."

"Sounds good to me," he replied.

For the next hour they went down the list of initials, filling in names as they came to mind and leaving the ones where names didn't immediately come.

They were more than halfway through the list when they came to the initials JF. "Perfect man Jackson is a JF."

"I can't imagine Jackson murdering anybody under any circumstances," she said, even as she typed his name into the spreadsheet.

"No, but he probably would have framed me to keep me away from you," Beau said wryly.

"Don't be ridiculous," she scoffed.

He laughed. "I'm not being ridiculous. You and I both know Jackson hated the fact that we were together."

"He still wouldn't have done anything like that," she replied. "Who else has those initials?" It took only a minute for her to think of another name. "Jason Farineau. He has money and clout, and I would guess he has little respect for his wife, so I can see him frequenting the women at the motel."

"Then there's Jack… Jack Fontenot," Beau added. "But at the time of the murder Jack wasn't married and our construction company had only just started. In fact, I'm seeing him Monday afternoon for a little business talk."

"He still goes on the list," she replied as she typed in his name.

They worked for another thirty minutes and then called it quits so she could run her errands. The first stop was Gravois's office, where Beau waited in the car while Peyton ran into the police station.

"Where did this come from?" Gravois asked when she handed him a copy of the initials.

"It doesn't matter. What matters is we believe these initials are of the men who saw Lacy around the time of her death. And we believe one of those men is her real killer."

He tossed the paper aside and frowned. "This is garbage. I don't know where you managed to dig that up, but it's not worth anything. Besides, do you really think I'm going to spend my time investigating a crime from fifteen years ago? There's plenty of crime happening right here and now that takes up all my time and energy."

His time and energy seemed to be mostly devoted to sitting at his desk and drinking coffee, she thought wryly. "I just thought you might want to know about this. You know, as one professional to another."

The stroke to his ego in identifying him as a fellow professional puffed out his chest. "I appreciate it, Peyton. I like to know what's going on in my town. Speaking of that...how'd you get that nasty bruise on your cheek?"

"A run-in with a cabinet door in the dark." The lie rolled easily off her tongue this time. There was no point in telling him the truth. He wouldn't be able to solve the crime of her attack without her being able to give him something to go on, and she had nothing. "And now I need to run," she said.

From Gravois's office, they went to city hall to get a list of all the tax-paying property owners in town and then they ended up in the bank, where she locked the original list into her safety deposit box.

"Why don't we head to Marie's and grab some dinner," he suggested once they were finished with all their running.

She looked at her watch, surprised that it was already almost six. The afternoon had flown by and as if to punctuate the point, her stomach growled loudly.

Beau laughed. "Now, that sounds like a woman ready to eat."

"And now that I think about it, I'm definitely hungry."

Kylie would have closed up the office so there

was really no reason not to grab dinner before heading home.

"It's Saturday night. Will we even be able to get a booth or a table?" she asked as Beau drove them toward the café.

"Marie will make sure we have a place to sit," he replied confidently.

Sure enough, the place was packed when they walked through the front doors. There were also several couples before them waiting to find an empty seat.

"Come on," Beau said. He grabbed her hand and pulled her back outside. "There's always a table in the kitchen for us."

"That was years ago, Beau. I'm sure things have changed by now," she replied.

He gazed at her with dark, enigmatic eyes. "Some things never change with time." He broke eye contact and led her around the building to the back door. When they walked in, Marie immediately spied them and hurried over to hug them both.

"We came to eat, but the place is packed," Beau said.

"You know you always have a table here," she said and pointed to the small table in the corner of the kitchen. "Sit, and then tell me what you want to eat."

They sat where they had years ago, with Marie beaming at the two of them. "Now, this brings me back to a happy place in life. Seeing you two together in my kitchen brings back all kinds of good memories," Marie said.

They ordered their food and while they waited, Peyton thought about Marie's words. Oh yes, there were wonderful memories here. She and Beau had spent many hours here in Marie's kitchen, enjoying the delicious food and laughing together.

This noisy, heavenly scented kitchen was a location where their love for each other had grown. They had teased each other and had long, meaningful discussions over platters of Marie's food. They had planned their future together, and those had been magical times.

She couldn't allow any of that magic to happen this time. Beau was a part of her past and she had no idea if he fit into her future or not. Aside from helping him clear his name, she wasn't at all sure what he wanted from her. Did he want anything more from her than a quick roll in the hay for old time's sake?

She knew instinctively that she couldn't fall in bed with him now and walk away unscathed. And the idea of making love to him again only to watch him walk away from her tortured her heart to its very depths.

Chapter Seven

Monday at one-thirty in the afternoon, Beau pulled his truck up to the curb in front of J's Construction Company. If the building front was any indication, the company had definitely done well in the past fifteen years. Painted a steel gray, the front of the business also boasted large black letters announcing the establishment. It appeared clean and classy, and a strong sense of pride filled him.

This had been his baby. Even at the young age of twenty-one, he knew the town had needed a new construction company with good, trustworthy and skilled workers.

He mourned for the time lost in being a part of this, in having the hands-on experiences of taking the company from its infancy to where it was now.

He'd called earlier that morning to make sure Jack would be in the office. Peyton also knew he'd be here this afternoon. He'd driven her to work that morning and just before she went into the building, she told him that she had a date that night with Sam Landry.

He'd been positively stunned by the news. For some reason he'd hoped she wouldn't be seeing the banker anymore.

He still didn't know what he really wanted from Peyton—although he definitely knew he wanted to make love to her one more time, if for no other reason than to get her completely out of his blood.

Knowing she had a date later tonight with Sam had kicked him in the ass. Sam was the antithesis of Beau. He was respectable and came from the same background as Peyton. He was a perfect match for her. Beau tried to shove all these thoughts aside as he walked up to the front door of the construction company.

A touch of anxiety filled his chest. He hoped like hell he could just walk back into the business and start working as soon as he finished up things with Peyton.

He opened the front door and stepped inside. The interior was huge, with samples of flooring and tile hanging on one side of the room. There was an area set up like a kitchen, with choices for color and back-splashes and miscellaneous other things. Finally, there was a huge wall of indoor/outdoor paint colors.

He found Jack seated at a desk in the back of the shop. "Hey, Beau." Jack stood and held out his hand.

Beau grasped Jack's hand firmly as he grinned at the man who had been his very best friend while growing up. "Good to see you again. Have a seat," Jack said once their handshake had ended.

Beau sank down in the chair in front of the desk, while Jack resumed his seat behind it. "The office looks amazing," Beau said. "Bigger and much better than I ever imagined."

"Yeah, it's finally all come together. How have you been adjusting to being back home?" Jack asked.

"I've been working a lot with Peyton. We're investigating Lacy's murder in order to find out the real killer. And speaking of Lacy… Did you ever visit her at the motel for any reason?"

"Never," he said firmly. "The day I have to pay for sex is the day I become celibate," he said with a laugh. "Besides, if you remember, I was dating Cecile Macron back then, and she was more than I could handle. Why would you ask me about seeing Lacy?"

"Just curious, that's all. So are you seeing anyone now?" Beau asked.

"I've been dating Mary Ingram for the last five months. In fact, I'm thinking about proposing to her in the very near future."

"I don't know her, but congratulations."

"She's a niece of Jimmy and Anne Ingram. Her parents were killed in a car crash when she was fifteen years old, and she came to live with them about a year after you got locked up. She's a nice woman who, for some strange reason, seems wild about me," Jack said with a wide grin.

"That's great, man," Beau replied.

"So you and Peyton have hooked up again. How's that going?" Jack asked.

"We haven't hooked up in any kind of a romantic way," Beau said. "We're just working together right now. And speaking of that, I'm here to talk about the business. I certainly don't expect you to pay me for all the time I was gone, but as part-owner, I would think I might be due something."

"Uh…" Jack glanced away from him. "Beau, you aren't a part-owner right now."

Beau looked at him in surprise. "What do you mean?"

Jack looked back at him with a deep frown. "Beau, you've got to look at all this from my position. You had been arrested for murder and convicted to spend years in prison. So I felt it was in my best interest— in the best interest of the company—to distance myself from you, so when I went to file the paperwork for the business, I didn't add you on as an owner."

Beau stared at him, stunned by what his friend had just told him. "So you cut me out even though the business was my idea and we had planned all of it as partners."

Jack's cheeks turned ruddy with color. "Hell, Beau, I didn't even know if I'd ever see you again. I had to do what was best for me. Why do you think I didn't write to you? I'm sorry, man, but that's just the way it is."

Beau stared at him for several long moments. "You believe I'm guilty," he finally said.

Once again Jack's cheeks turned red and he looked away from Beau. "I don't… I didn't know what to believe. All I knew was I couldn't have a business partner who was in prison for murder."

For fifteen years Beau had believed he had a business to come home to. That and thoughts of Peyton were what had kept him sane as he went through the long days and nights of prison life.

He was so shocked by this turn of events, for several long moments he didn't know what to say or how to act. He finally managed to pull himself together. "I'm hoping to clear my name in the next month or two. Once I do that, can we revisit this issue?"

"Sure, we can do that, but I really don't see how you're going to solve a crime that happened so long ago," Jack replied.

"We've gotten a major clue and so we're hoping it will help us find the real killer in the next week or so," Beau replied.

"Really? What's the clue?" Jack asked curiously.

"We're keeping it close to our chests until the time we can name our killer," Beau replied and stood. "So I guess I'll just see you around."

"Beau, I'm sorry for the way things turned out," Jack said.

"Yeah, me, too."

"Once you clear your name then come back to see me and we'll talk about the business again."

Beau didn't reply but rather turned and headed for the door. He felt as if his very guts had just been punched out of him.

He didn't understand why Jack hadn't, at the very

least, considered Beau a silent partner and put his name on the paperwork as one of the owners. If he was worried about Beau's name being tied to the business, nobody would have had to know that he was a silent partner. It wasn't like Jack had to flash his paperwork every time he did a job.

It was a deep cut, an ultimate betrayal by the man he'd once considered his very best friend. Jack had been like a brother to Beau, but right now Beau felt like he'd been gutted.

Once outside, he got into his truck but instead of heading directly back toward Peyton's office, he drove aimlessly up and down the streets.

Initially, he'd come up with the idea of a construction company because Black Bayou only had a couple of handymen to take care of the needs of the people. More importantly, it had been something he'd wanted to do in order to make himself more worthy of Peyton.

Peyton's family was wealthy, and he'd wanted to be able to bring something to the table to prove to them that he was more than just a swamp rat. He wanted to prove to them that he could provide for Peyton in a respectable, meaningful way.

When he'd come back here after serving time, he'd been oddly pleased to discover that Peyton was still single. He'd believed he'd walk back into his business and he'd take time to explore his unresolved feelings where she was concerned.

However, while Peyton was helping him, she wasn't

really letting him into her life in any meaningful way. Hell, she had a date tonight! And now his business had basically been stolen away from him. At the moment he felt more broken than the day he'd been pronounced guilty in Lacy's murder.

He now realized he had nothing here. Even if he cleared his name, he wasn't sure he was willing to go to Jack and beg and grovel for a piece of the business back. He'd thought he knew what his future held, but now he had no clue. Even if they managed to clear his name, he had no idea going forward what he would do for work.

He drove around for about an hour and then finally found himself parked in front of the Voodoo Lounge. It was a dive bar on the west side of town, a place his father had frequented often.

Being raised by a mean alcoholic father, Beau had sworn he'd never grow up to be a drunk like his old man, but right now a drink called to him to take the edge off the raw emotions that roared through him…myriad emotions he couldn't begin to untangle at the moment.

He walked into the dim premises that smelled of stale beer, perspiration and greasy bar food. There were several men seated at the long bar, not speaking to each other but instead staring down into their drinks.

Beau moved to the far end of the bar, not wanting to interact with anyone. He was not in the mood to make friendly chatter. All he wanted was a scotch on the rocks and a few minutes to process where on earth he was going with his life, with his future.

He ordered from the bartender, a young man he didn't know, and once he had the drink in hand, he took a deep sip of it, welcoming the slide of warmth down his throat and into his stomach.

It felt as if all he'd ever known in his entire life was carpentry and Peyton, and he now realized for the first time since being back in Black Bayou that it didn't matter whether he was innocent or not... he was going to have to rebuild his life from the ground up.

Without carpentry...and without Peyton.

He slammed down the rest of the drink and then ordered another one. He sipped this one slowly, staring down at the scars on the bar top. Initials carved into the wood were next to drink rings and cigarette burns.

What in the hell was he doing here? In a dive bar where losers who had given up on themselves came to die a slow death? Dammit, he wasn't a loser. He was a survivor. He didn't belong here.

He needed to get out of there. He checked the time on his phone and realized it was a few minutes before four. Peyton had wanted to go home by three so he was late getting back to take her home.

He pushed the second drink away and then left the bar. As he drove back to Peyton's office, a slow burn of anger reignited in the pit of his stomach.

It was anger at the utter betrayal by the friend he

had trusted more than any other man, and by the woman who had once declared her undying love for him, yet had still believed him capable of killing a woman.

It was slow-burning rage at a life that had seen him tossed into prison for a crime he hadn't committed, of having so much of his life stolen from him.

By the time he pulled up to Peyton's office, his anger still clung to him like a layer of Spanish moss hugging a cypress tree.

When he entered the building there was no sign of Kylie at the front desk. Peyton opened the inner office door and stepped out.

"You're late," she said, her tone holding more than a little bit of irritation.

He stepped closer to her. "Does it really take you this much time to get ready for your big date with Mr. Wonderful Sam?"

She frowned. "Don't be a jerk about it, Beau. Sam is a very nice man and I asked you to be back here to get me home by three today. I texted you several times."

He took another step toward her. "I didn't pay attention to the texts and I'm not being a jerk about Sam. I see how perfect he is for you. He comes from the right background, he's highly respectable... On paper he ticks all the boxes for being the perfect husband for you."

"What on earth gave you the idea I'm looking for a husband?"

"I don't know. I know how much you wanted children and time is a ticking." This time his step forward put him so close to her he could smell her tantalizing scent and see the slight whisper of something in the depths of her eyes. "Don't you remember, *ma chérie*, how we planned for our babies? First, a little boy and then a baby girl? Perhaps you were just pretending to want my children. Maybe you were just pretending the whole time to love me."

Her eyes flared wide and she pushed hard against his chest, moving him back a step. "You've been drinking," she said with surprised accusation.

"Ah, give the lady a stuffed bear," he replied sarcastically and clapped his hands together.

"Beau, what are you trying to do right now? Why do I get the distinct feeling you're trying to pick a fight with me?" Her beautiful eyes searched his features.

Just that quickly his anger seeped out of him, leaving a bad taste in the back of his mouth. He looked away from her and took several more steps back. "Don't worry about it. Let's get you home."

The drive to her place was silence and charged with tension. Once they arrived, she got out of the truck and slammed the door behind her. He headed back to Vincent's and then he headed back into the swamp. As he ran through the thick vegetation, he wondered if he'd been a fool all along to believe he could have a life outside the swamp.

Maybe, like Angel, he was destined to live all alone in his shack, picking up odd jobs here and there to make enough money to sustain him.

He'd definitely been a fool to believe he would get the girl, because his girl was now getting ready for a date with another man.

THAT EVENING WAS Peyton's last date with Sam. At the end of the date, after dinner at the café, she'd told Sam they had no future together and should stop seeing one another.

They had dated enough times now that she knew she had no real physical attraction to him. It wasn't fair for her to keep going on dinner dates with him. It wasn't fair to keep wasting his time when she felt the way she did about him. He was a nice man, but he wasn't her man.

She and Beau had worked every afternoon to make sure they had all the names matched up with the initials. She'd checked the tax records to find names there and as of this morning they had twenty-three men on their list, one of whom was assuredly Lacy's killer.

As she stared down at the names, a banging began from outside. Beau had finished up yanking off all the rotten wood from the front of the building three days ago. The next day she'd arranged for a delivery of some of the new supplies he would need to continue the job, and he'd gotten straight to work.

Beau. For the past week she'd been a bit concerned about him. Since the day he'd come back to the office late after having a drink or two and then taken her home, he'd been unusually quiet and distant.

Gone was the wicked sparkle in his eyes, along with the seductive overtures from him. She'd told herself she hated it when he reached out and touched her hair or stroked his fingers down her cheeks. But the truth of the matter was she missed all those things now.

More importantly, she wanted to know what had happened to change things with him. Was he still reacting to the fact that she'd had a date with Sam? She hadn't told him yet that she'd broken things off with Sam, but he'd known she was seeing the banker from the very beginning of this strange working new relationship of theirs.

So if it wasn't that, then what was it? What had changed in him? And why did she miss him teasing and tormenting her with his sinful words and touch?

She shoved these troubling thoughts aside. On the agenda for today was going to see Louis Rivet, the alcoholic whose testimony had helped to put Beau away.

In the excitement of getting Lacy's note from the grave, she'd nearly forgotten what else needed to be done in order to prove Beau's innocence.

It was a long shot that the man would remember anything meaningful about that night so long ago, but she couldn't leave any stone unturned in their pursuit of the truth.

She spent the morning reading over the paperwork she had generated for the case of Beau's innocence. She checked and double-checked the names on their list of potential suspects. She'd been surprised to discover that several of the men whose initials were on Lacy's list of clients were also "happily" married pillars of society.

Once they spoke with Louis, then they would begin interviewing the men on their list and hopefully, the real killer would somehow give them a sign of their guilt.

They had already written off a few of the men on the list, such as Jack Fontenot, who was Beau's business partner. At the time of Lacy's death, he'd been a young man just talking about starting up a business. Neither Peyton nor Beau saw him as a potential blackmail subject.

She'd wanted to write off Jackson, not wanting to believe her good friend could have had anything to do with the murder. Even though Jackson had been a young man, too, at the time of Lacy's murder, his hefty bank account along with his hatred of Beau gave her pause.

Was it possible Jackson had been seeing Lacy? Was it somehow possible he had found Beau's necklace and had decided to remove Beau from Peyton's life? Her heart told her there was no way Jackson would murder a woman, but her head couldn't write him off completely.

The morning seemed to fly by. The banging outside eventually stopped, she ate a sandwich for lunch, and then around one Beau walked into her office. He smelled of clean male, letting her know he'd taken a shower after working in the heat all morning.

"Are you ready to go?" he asked.

"Yes, I'm ready." She pulled her purse from beneath her desk and stood.

Together they left the inner office and Peyton smiled at Kylie. "We're heading out for a while. You know the drill, keep the doors open and if anyone comes in, have them fill out a contact form. We should be back before five, but if we aren't just close up as usual."

"Got it," Kylie replied with her usual bright smile.

Minutes later they were in Beau's truck and headed toward the motel, where Louis still lived in the unit two doors down from the room where Lacy had once lived and had been murdered.

"I still can't believe Louis was the prosecutor's main witness," she said.

"Gravois would have taken a statement from a sunbathing gator if he thought it would help put me away," Beau replied dryly. "Sometimes I wonder if he knows who the real killer is—if he got a payoff or something in order for him to protect the guilty."

"I would certainly hate to believe that of our law

enforcement, especially that the chief of police would actually cover up for a murderer."

"I'd believe anything when it comes to Gravois," he replied darkly.

"Well, let's hope Louis remembers something more from that night than seeing you go into Lacy's room and then leave." What she wanted to do was ask Beau what had changed between them. Why had he been so distant lately?

However, this wasn't the place and there wasn't enough time to have any kind of a real discussion with him as before she knew it, he was pulling into the motel parking lot. There was a part of her that was reluctant to say anything at all and just hoped he resolved whatever was going on in his head.

He parked in front of unit five, where a faded red beat-up fishing chair sat just outside the door. They got out of the car and Beau walked up to the unit. He knocked and they waited a moment but there was no answer. He knocked a little harder with the same response.

"Maybe he isn't here," she said.

"Oh, he's here. No self-respecting drunk is seen out and about this early in the day." He banged on the door with enough force to wake the dead.

"Wha…what's going on?" Louis's voice bellowed from inside.

"Louis, we need to speak with you," Peyton yelled through the door.

"Are you the cops?" Louis asked.

"No, we aren't the cops," Peyton replied and wondered why he would be expecting the police.

"Give me just a minute." It took more like five minutes before Louis's door finally opened. Instantly, the smell of booze filled the air. Louis's short legs were clad in a pair of dirty jeans. His protruding stomach was covered with a filthy white T-shirt, and his gray hair was a grizzly mass that looked like it hadn't seen a comb in years.

At one point in his life, Peyton had heard that Louis was a fine car mechanic. Unfortunatly booze had stolen not only his job away from him, but also his home and everything else.

He frowned first at Beau and then at Peyton. "Who are you and what in the hell do you want with me?"

"My name is Peyton LaCroix and I'm a defense attorney. I'm here to talk to you about the murder that took place here fifteen years ago."

Louis's frown deepened. "I don't ever like to think about that. It was the very worst night of my life. It makes me so sad. She was such a nice woman. Sometimes she would bring me a sandwich."

"I know it was sad, Louis, but I really need you to think about that night right now," Peyton replied.

Louis's dark eyes gazed at her slyly. "I always think a little better if I have a bit of cash in my pocket."

Peyton started to open her purse, but Beau stopped

her. "No. We don't pay for information," he said firmly to Louis.

Louis glared at Beau for several long moments and then his eyes widened and he released a small gasp. "You're him… I saw you that night going into her room."

"That's right. This is Beau Boudreau. He was a good friend of Lacy's. Do you have any idea what time you saw him go into her room?" Peyton asked.

"Don't you remember?" Louis asked Beau.

"We need *you* to remember," Peyton said.

"Let me think a minute." He unfolded the fishing chair and sank down and as he did, she noticed that his hands held a slight tremor. He'd just awakened and he was probably already in withdrawal.

"I was sitting here that night, enjoying a little cocktail or two and watching the people come and go," he said. He frowned again. "That was a long time ago."

"Yes, I know it was, but I really need you to think about it, Louis," Peyton pressed. "It's important. Was it after dark when Beau came here?"

His bushy eyebrows pulled together in another frown. "I'm thinking it was around sunset."

Beau nodded and Peyton continued, "So did you see anyone else come to her room that night?"

He darted a glance to the left and to the right, and then looked back at Peyton. "They told me not to tell about anyone else coming," Louis replied in a whisper.

Peyton's heart banged against her ribs in an accelerated beat. "Who told you that, Louis? Who told
you not to say anything about other people coming
to her room?"

"Gravois and that other man, the one who bought
me a new suit."

"You mean Charles Landry, the former prosecuting attorney?"

Louis nodded. "That's him. He bought me a nice,
new suit and then let me stay with him in his big old
mansion for two nights before the trial. It was luxury
digs, that's for sure. The bed was so soft I felt like I
was sleeping on a cloud."

"Back to my original question," Peyton continued. "Did you see anyone else visit Lacy's room on
the night of her murder?"

"She had a couple more visitors that night after
Beau left. But don't ask me who they were because
it was dark and I didn't really see them clearly. Are
we done now?"

"Almost," Peyton replied. "Did Lacy's other visitors that night drive here?"

"They did. You'd be surprised by how many fancy
cars used to creep in here under the cover of night,"
Louis replied.

"Did you recognize what kind of cars the visitors
drove in?" Peyton asked.

"Nah, I don't know much about cars. They all look
alike to me, especially when it's dark outside. But
they were fancy ones."

"I am absolutely outraged by what we just heard," Peyton said a few minutes later as Beau left the motel parking lot. "Gravois and Landry paid a witness to forget what he saw. They bribed him with a new suit and a stay in *luxurious digs*. With that information alone I could get you a new trial, Beau. You go back to trial and I know we could win and clear your name."

"I don't care about a new trial, and I'm not sure I care about any of this anymore."

She shot him a look of surprise. "What are you talking about? Beau, what's wrong?"

"Nothing's wrong. But I was wondering if I could just take you on home now. I know it's early, but I have some other things to take care of and I don't want you getting home from the office under your own steam."

"I guess I could go on home for the day," she agreed. "But we go on as usual tomorrow, right?"

He was silent for a long moment and then released a deep sigh. "I guess," he finally agreed.

"You can't give up on this now, Beau," she said fervently. "I don't know what's going on in that brain of yours right now, but you can't give up on finding out the truth. I really believe we're moving closer and closer to learning the answers that will finally set you free and see a killer behind bars."

By that time, he had pulled up in her driveway. She placed her hand on his arm and felt a simmering tension there. "Promise me, Beau. Promise me that we don't stop digging until we have the answers about who really killed Lacy. She deserves justice."

Once again, he was quiet for several long moments. He finally looked at her, but his eyes were shuttered and revealed nothing of his thoughts. He looked at her for just a moment and then gazed back out the truck window. "Okay, I promise," he replied.

"Then I'll see you in the morning." She got out of the truck and then went into her house, her thoughts deeply troubled. Why was she suddenly fighting harder for Beau's innocence than he was? Dammit, what had changed with him?

The first thing she did was call Kylie and let her know she was going to be out of the office for the rest of the day. Once that was done, she decided to indulge herself with a leisurely bath.

Fifteen minutes later she lowered herself into the tub full of warm water and scented bubbles. Immediately, thoughts of Beau once again filled her head.

Why on earth would he be ready to give up on finding the killer when each day she felt them getting closer to discovering the murderer's identity? Once again she was reminded that she really didn't know this Beau. She'd only known him as a confident, bold young man. This brooding, quiet man was a virtual stranger to her.

She remained in the tub until the water turned cold and all the bubbles were gone and only then did she get out. She dried off and then pulled on a pink sleeveless summer shift.

She ate a salad for dinner and then curled up on the sofa to watch a little television. It felt good to give herself the permission to stop thinking about anything important for a little while and instead just enjoy watching several silly sitcoms.

When it finally got dark outside, she was drowsy and ready to call it a night. She turned off the television and pulled herself up and off the sofa.

Before heading to her bedroom, she walked over to her front window to pull the curtains closed. Normally, she did that as soon as she got home from work, but with her normal schedule being disrupted that day, she'd forgotten to do it.

She now reached out for one side of the gray curtain and pulled it closed. She turned, but before she could walk away a boom sounded from outside. The window glass exploded inward and at the same time a scorching pain seared through her shoulder.

She stumbled backward and fell to the floor. *Wha...what just happened?* For a moment her brain refused to work as pain flamed through her.

She was afraid to stand and so she began to crawl toward the kitchen, where her purse was on the counter. Sobs escaped her...deep sobs of both fear and pain. She needed her cell phone. Oh, God, she needed to call somebody for help.

Shock ripped through her as she tried to process what had just happened to her. As she moved, bright red blood splashed on the floor from the wound in her shoulder.

She finally got to her purse, yanked out her cell phone and called for help. "This is Peyton LaCroix," she said amid sobs to the emergency dispatcher. "Please, I n-need help. I've j-just been shot."

Chapter Eight

Beau sat on his sofa and listened to the bog singing its nighttime songs. He felt as if he'd been in a fog ever since speaking with Jack. He wasn't sure it mattered anymore whether he proved his innocence or not. Sure, it would be great to find the real killer, the person who had not only snuffed out Lacy's life but also framed him for the crime. But after speaking with Jack, he'd lost his vision of returning to a productive and meaningful life here.

He'd spent most of his adult life as an inmate. He'd been told when and what to eat, when to go to work and when to sleep. Now without his business to go back to, he felt absolutely rudderless.

As a carpenter on his own he would never be able to compete with the business Jack now had. He still wanted to build something for himself career-wise, but he didn't know where to begin.

And then there was Peyton...

"Yo, Beau." The deep voice came from outside.

Beau jumped up and opened his door. Gator stood

just outside. "Hey, Gator. What's going on? Out on one of your nighttime walks?"

"I was, but while I was walking, I figured you'd want to hear what I just now heard through the grapevine," the old man said.

"And what's that?" Beau asked.

"I just heard that your lady friend lawyer got shot tonight."

"Got shot?" Beau stared at Gator for a long moment as his brain whirled to make sense of what he'd just heard. "Shot..." he echoed faintly. "Where... Is she okay?"

"I don't know anything else about it other than she was shot and rushed to the hospital. I figured you needed to know."

Energy flooded through Beau. "Thanks, Gator." Beau turned around and went back inside, where he grabbed the truck keys. He then raced back outside, passing by Gator as Beau raced through the swamp to get to where his truck was parked.

The grapevine in the swamp was usually fairly accurate, but in this case he desperately hoped it was wrong. If the gossip was right, then how badly had she been hurt? Where had she been to get shot in the first place?

A hundred questions raced through his head and his heart was beating a million miles a minute when he finally reached his truck. He jumped inside, fired up the engine and took off for the hospital.

If she wasn't there, then he would know the gossip had been wrong. He prayed she wasn't there and that she was in her home safe and sound.

He tightened his hands on the steering wheel as he sped down the streets. He still couldn't figure out where she'd been if she'd really gotten shot. Had she decided to make a quick run to the grocery store? To another store? Dammit, how could he protect her if she decided to go out and about on her own?

He finally squealed into the hospital lot and pulled into one of the empty parking spaces. He cut the engine, got out of his truck and then raced for the emergency room entrance.

Lydia March manned the desk. He'd known her before he'd gone to prison. They had gone to school together. Her eyes now widened slightly at the sight of him. "Hey, Beau."

"Hi, Lydia. I heard Peyton LaCroix was brought in a little while ago for a gunshot wound. Could you tell the doctor I'm here and would like to know her condition as soon as possible?"

She nodded. "I'll be right back." She disappeared through a door that was marked Authorized Personnel Only.

Beau's heart dropped. He'd hoped that Lydia would look at him like he was out of his mind and tell him Peyton wasn't here. But she hadn't, which meant Peyton was here and she had really been shot.

So how badly had she been hurt? Was she now barely clinging to life? How had this happened? The thought nearly cast him to his knees. He walked over to one of the plastic chairs and collapsed down, his heart still beating a rhythm of anxiety.

Lydia returned to the desk. "Dr. Richards will be with you when he can."

"Thanks," Beau replied.

He remained seated in the chair for what seemed like an eternity. His heart continued to beat an unnatural quickened rhythm as he prayed that she would be okay.

Finally, Dr. Richards came through the door. Beau jumped up out of his chair to greet the doctor. He had no memory of the dark-haired man who appeared to be about Beau's age.

"She's doing just fine," Dr. Richards said. "She gave me permission to speak to you. She's one lucky lady—the bullet only grazed her shoulder. She heard you were here and she wants to see you. I'll take you back to her."

A wealth of relief shuddered through Beau as he followed the doctor through the door that led into the emergency room treatment area. He turned into the first unit and Beau stepped in behind him.

She sat in the bed, appearing small and fragile. She was clad in a hospital gown and it was obvious her right shoulder wore thick bandages.

The moment she saw Beau she burst into tears. He rushed to her side, wanting to pull her into his arms and hold her there forever, but he was afraid of further hurting her. Instead, he leaned over, kissed her forehead and then took hold of her left hand.

"S…somebody shot me, Beau. Somebody shot me right through my living room window," she said amid her tears. "I… I was getting ready to…to pull my curtains closed and somebody shot me."

"I'm sorry, chérie. I'm so sorry this happened to you, but you're safe now," he said softly. He wanted to hear exactly what happened, but first he looked at the doctor. "What happens next?"

"She's free to go. I've cleaned and dressed the wound and given her some pain medication. I'll write a prescription for some antibiotics and pain pills. If you both just sit tight, I'll take care of that and then send the nurse in."

"Thank you, Doctor," Beau said.

"Yes, thank you for taking such good care of me," Peyton added through her tears.

Once the doctor was gone, Beau pulled a chair up next to the side of Peyton's bed. "It's all my fault," she said and grabbed a tissue from the box on the table next to her. She dabbed at her teary eyes.

"How is this your fault?" he asked.

"I made myself the perfect target." She explained to him how she'd forgotten to pull the curtains shut when she'd first arrived home. "When I decided to close them, I made a perfect target in the window. It…it was stupid of me."

Beau frowned. What bothered him was the fact that somebody had obviously been outside her house just waiting for the exact opportunity to shoot her.

And he had a definite feeling this wasn't her fault, but rather it was his.

He should have never pulled her into his desire to catch a killer. After she was attacked next to her car and punched in the face, he should have walked away from her.

Before he could voice his thoughts to her, Thomas Gravois stepped into the room. "Peyton, how are you doing?"

"I'm okay, considering I was just shot," she said with a touch of sarcasm. She grabbed the button to raise the head of the hospital bed a little more. "Thankfully, the bullet just grazed my shoulder."

"Well, that's good. I wish I could tell you we've got the shooter under arrest, but unfortunately, we don't." The lawman pulled a pen and a small notebook out of his back pocket. "I didn't get a chance to talk to you before the ambulance took you away, so now I need to know exactly what happened."

As Peyton relayed the events of the night, Beau's brain whirled with dozens of thoughts. The fact that if the bullet had hit her an inch or so to the left, then she'd be dead, absolutely horrified him.

Who? Who had sat in a vehicle or stood outside in her yard with the intent of killing her? He didn't have to ask himself the *why*. He suspected whoever it was believed that if Peyton was dead then Beau would be so distraught, he'd be so ripped apart, that he'd stop his quest for the killer. And that was probably what would happen.

He'd be devastated if Peyton died, not because he needed her to help him clear his name. Despite his core of hurt and anger at her for not believing in him years ago, he still cared deeply about her.

He focused back on the conversation between Peyton and Gravois. "We canvassed the area and spoke to your neighbors. Unfortunately, none of them saw a person or a vehicle in front of your place. So they were no help in identifying the shooter," Gravois said.

"That doesn't surprise me," Pcyton said. "It was dark outside and there aren't enough streetlights in the area to begin with."

"The good news is we found the slug in the wall opposite the front window. I'll send it off to the lab to see what they can tell me about it."

"Hell, everyone in this town owns a gun. It's going to be damned hard to match the striations and whatever to a gun unless that particular gun was used in another crime," Beau said.

"Do you know anyone who might have an issue with you?" Gravois asked her. "Maybe somebody who was unhappy with your representation in a particular case?"

"I can tell you who did this. It's the same person who punched her in the face," Beau said. "It's Lacy Dupree's murderer. He feels the heat of us getting closer to him and he's getting desperate to somehow halt our investigation."

"When did somebody punch you in the face?"

Gravois asked, a deep frown cutting across his forehead. "Is that how you got that bruise that was on your face? You told me you ran into a cabinet door."

"It's not important now," Peyton replied. "I didn't see the person at all so I didn't report it because I knew there was nothing you could do about it."

"Still, you should have made a report. I need to know what's happening in my town."

"Speaking of what's going on in your town, have there been any breaks in the Honey Island Monster murders?" Beau asked.

"We're working on it," Gravois said, his frown cutting even deeper. He looked back at Peyton. "We finished up our investigation in your house so you're free to go home whenever you get released from here. I left an officer there to guard it since it was unlocked and we didn't know if you had a key."

"Actually, I'm being released in just a few minutes," she replied. "And I didn't exactly take the time to grab my house keys."

"Peyton, I want you to know I'm taking this all very seriously and will continue to work the case." Gravois shoved his pen and notepad back into his pocket. "In the meantime, the two of you might want to consider halting your little investigation. You're both just asking for trouble."

"Thanks for the advice," Peyton said. "But somebody has to investigate to find the real killer, and you've made it abundantly clear that you just want to forget that an innocent man went to prison."

Gravois's nostrils flared with his displeasure at her words. "I have more than enough on my plate right now. I don't have the time or the energy to go back and re-solve a crime that happened fifteen years ago. In the meantime, I'll stay in touch and if anything else happens, don't hesitate to call me."

The minute Gravois left, a nurse came into the room. "Here are your two scripts." She handed the two pieces of paper to Peyton. "And here's clean bandages for your wound. The doctor wants your bandages changed tomorrow. Unfortunately, the pretty shift you wore in didn't survive, so you'll have to wear the hospital gown home. Now, let's get that IV out of you and you can be on your way."

Forty-five minutes later they had picked up her two prescriptions and were pulling up in Peyton's driveway. He got out of the truck and then hurried around to help her out.

A single police officer sat in a car by the curb. He got out of his vehicle and approached them. "The front door was left unlocked so Chief Gravois directed me to sit on the house until you returned here."

"Thank you so much," Peyton said. "I appreciate being able to go back inside and not be afraid that somebody is in there waiting for me."

"Trust me. Nobody is inside, but if it would make you feel better, I could do a quick walk-through."

"Do you mind?"

"Not at all. Why don't you two wait out here for a couple of minutes and I'll check out the premises."

"I hate this," Beau said as the officer disappeared into the house. "I hate that this has happened and I hate that I'm not the man with a gun going in to check things out. But as a felon, I can't own a gun. And I hate like hell that this happened to you." A swift anger filled him, but he tamped it down. Peyton didn't need his anger right now.

He reached out to her and pulled her closer to him, careful not to hurt her shoulder. To his surprise, she came willingly into him. "I own a gun," she said softly.

Before Beau could respond, the police officer came back outside. "All clear," he said.

"Thank you," Peyton said and moved away from Beau.

"No problem. I hope we catch the creep. I'm just sorry this happened to you, Ms. LaCroix, and now I need to be on my way."

A moment later the officer was gone and Beau and Peyton walked into her living room. Glass shards glittered on the floor near the window. Beau stepped over the mess to close the curtains and then he turned to face her.

"Are you ready to stop now and leave things up to me?" he asked.

"Hell no," she replied, and that stubborn chin of hers shot straight up. "This just makes me angrier and even more determined than ever to catch this creep. Among his other crimes, he tried to kill me tonight. I just need to be more careful."

"You aren't safe here anymore, Peyton. Don't you understand that? You can no longer stay here, but I know a place where you'll be perfectly safe. Go change your clothes and pack a bag. I'm taking you to the swamp."

PEYTON STARED AT Beau in utter shock. She immediately wanted to protest the very idea, but despite her bravado, there was no denying that she was still shaken up by what had happened here tonight.

She'd been shot, and there was absolutely no question in her mind that it had been attempted murder. There was also no question in her mind that there was a very strong possibility the person would try to kill her again.

The idea of being someplace where she wouldn't be afraid, where she could just take a little time to rest and to heal and to feel safe, sounded wonderfully appealing. She knew she would have all that at Beau's place.

"Okay, just for a couple of days," she finally said. "I'll go change and pack."

"Do you have anything in your garage that I could use to board up this missing window?" he asked.

"I think there might be some plywood scraps out in the garage," she replied.

"You go pack and I'll see what I can do."

She nodded and then went into her bedroom as he headed for the garage. At least the blinds in her room were pulled tightly closed so nobody could see in.

The pain in her shoulder was beyond intense and the whole night felt like a horrible nightmare. She was exhausted, but knew she wouldn't be able to sleep peacefully here in her own bed, for at least the next night or two.

Thankfully, yesterday morning Irene Farineau's shoplifting case had come to an end when the prosecuting attorney had suddenly decided to drop all the charges against her. Peyton suspected some sort of a cash settlement had taken place behind the scenes. In any case, what that meant for her was that she had nothing pending at the office, so she could take off for a couple of days.

She'd call Kylie in the morning and give her a couple days off. She hoped the young woman wasn't in any danger and Peyton didn't really believe she was. Still, at this very moment all she could really think about was getting someplace to take a pain pill and lie down.

She packed a few things in a backpack and at the last minute tucked her gun inside even though she didn't believe the person they were after, the person who was after her, would venture into the swamp to find them. She certainly didn't believe anyone would come into the swamp and discover Beau was around a gun.

She heard some banging coming from the living room and realized Beau was working to cover the broken window. Finally, she changed into a pair of jeans and, with some pain and difficulty, a T-shirt, and then walked back out into the living room where Beau was once again seated on the sofa and the window was covered with a large sheet of plywood. He jumped up from the sofa and took the backpack from her. "Ready to go?"

"As ready as I can be." She grabbed her purse off the kitchen floor where she'd dropped it after she'd made the call for help. "Thanks for taking care of the window."

"No problem," he replied. "It will work until you make arrangements to have a new window installed."

Together they stepped out of the house. She locked the door and then they returned to Beau's truck. "How are you feeling?" he asked softly once they were on their way.

"Like I'm more than ready for a pain pill and some sleep," she admitted.

"Peyton, I'm so sorry you're in pain. I wish I could take it all away from you. I wish somehow that I could erase this entire night." His soft voice, coupled with the warm gaze he shot her way, unexpectedly pulled tears to her eyes.

She swallowed hard against them and closed her eyes. She leaned her head back and released a deep sigh. It was silly, now that it was all over and she was safe, but a deep fear still swept through her. Maybe it was just because she was in so much pain.

However, there was no question that she felt safer with Beau by her side. "I'll need to call to get the glass in my window replaced," she said. "And I also need to contact my homeowner's insurance."

"None of that needs to be done tonight," Beau replied. "Tonight you just take your medicine and rest."

They drove for several more minutes and she only opened her eyes again when the truck stopped. They were parked in the lot by the little grocery store and ahead was the path that would eventually lead to Beau's place.

He got her bag out of the bed of the truck and strapped it on his back, and she grabbed her purse tightly in one of her hands. "Baby, I wish I could carry you in, but that's just not possible," he said.

"I know... I'll be fine as long as you hold my hand," she replied. There was no way she could navigate the swamp darkness without his help.

He reached out and clasped his hand firmly around hers. "Let's go," he said.

They entered the marsh and he walked slowly, murmuring softly to tell her where to step in order to avoid thick roots or the dark water that shimmered around them in the faint moonlight.

The deeper they went in, the cooler the air around them. It was always far cooler in the swamp. They passed several other paths that went elsewhere and continued on.

Nobody who didn't know the swamp would be able to find Beau's place. She would bet on the fact that her attacker hadn't come from here, but rather he was a townsman who had plenty to lose if their investigation identified him. And townspeople never, ever ventured into the swamp.

By the time they reached Beau's place, her shoulder throbbed painfully and tears once again filled her eyes. She felt physically and emotionally broken and she hated herself for her weakness.

"Wait here," he said when they finally reached his front door. He went inside the dark structure, and a few moments later he'd turned on two lanterns that gave the main room a soft glow.

He walked back over to where she stood and took her by the hand. "Come... Sit on the sofa and I'll get you one of your pain pills and an antibiotic and some water."

She sank down on the sofa and watched as he pulled a jug of water out of the icebox and poured a liberal amount into a glass. She pulled the prescriptions out of her purse, and he approached with the water glass. "Here, you take this and I'll take those."

They made the exchange and then he shook out one pill from each of the bottles and handed them to her. She swallowed them, set her glass on the coffee table and then released a deep, weary sigh.

"This whole night has been nothing but a nightmare," she said. "I still can't believe somebody was outside my house just waiting for the perfect opportunity to shoot me."

"Yeah, I can't believe it, either." She heard the frustration in his voice. His gaze lingered on her for a long moment. "And thank God that bullet only grazed your shoulder. When I thought about what could have happened it makes me sick."

She gave him a tired smile. "It makes me a little sick, too."

For the next few minutes they discussed the events of the night. "I think you're done for now," he said with a smile to her. "Your pain pill must be working because you not only look drowsy, but you're also slurring your words a little bit."

"I am feeling it," she admitted.

"I'm sure you're ready for some sleep," he said. "You can take the bedroom and I'll sleep out here on the sofa," he said.

"Thank you, Beau. If you don't mind, I am ready to go to bed." She rose and grabbed her purse as he picked up her backpack and carried it into the bedroom.

He went in first and turned on a lantern on the nightstand. "I've only slept on the sheets for two nights, but I'd be glad to change them if you want me to," he said and set the backpack on the foot of the bed.

"That's not necessary. I just need a day or two to heal a bit and then I'll be out of your hair," she replied.

"We'll see about that," he said. "If you need anything just let me know." He walked over to her and gently kissed her on her forehead. "You're safe here, Peyton. I would wrestle a ticked-off gator to keep you safe."

She offered him a faint smile. "Then let's pray that no angry gators come knocking at your door."

"Is there anything else you need?" he asked.

"No, I'm good."

"Good night, Peyton," he said and then pulled the bedroom door closed behind him.

She got her nightgown out of the bag and, with some painful difficulty, got out of her T-shirt and bra and into the nightwear. She then pulled her jeans off and placed them and the T-shirt across the dresser.

Her phone in her purse would stay charged for another six to ten hours or so and then it would be dead and she had no idea whether there was a way to charge it out here or not. For once in her life, she wouldn't mind it going dead. There was nobody she really needed to talk to, and the downtime was just what she needed.

Finally, she crawled into the double bed. Instantly, she was enveloped by Beau's unique scent. She left the lantern lit and stared at the shadows that danced across the ceiling.

It was here, in this room, in this very bed, that she'd lost her virginity years before. That night the white-hot passion she'd felt for Beau had finally exploded and they had taken their relationship to a new level.

She knew that had been a long time ago. But she'd always felt safe and protected here with Beau, and that was still true tonight.

It didn't take long for the pain in her shoulder to

ease to a dull throb and a deep drowsiness to overtake her. She rolled over on her side and turned off the lantern, plunging the room into complete darkness.

The sound of the swamp filled the room...the slap of fish...the croaking of frogs...myriad sounds that created a soft lullaby, and soon she heard nothing at all as sleep claimed her.

Chapter Nine

Beau awoke early the next morning and his first thought was of the woman who slept in his bedroom. She had never spent the night here in the swamp before. Years ago, when they had been young lovers, he'd always walked her out of the swamp and to her home in the middle of the night.

She didn't know it yet, but he intended to keep her here until the danger to her was over. That meant she'd be here until they identified the person who had attacked her, the person he believed was the real murderer of Lacy. That meant she was going to be here longer than a day or two.

He had a feeling that it was far too late for him to try to disassociate from her. She was already in too deep with him and the investigation. The killer would probably still go after her no matter how loud and long Beau denounced their partnership.

The only thing Beau needed to do right now was keep her here, where she would be safe, for as long as possible. While she remained here, he would continue to work the case alone.

He got up from the sofa and built a fire in the stove. Once Peyton was awake, he'd cook some breakfast for them both. With the fire burning, he went to the bedroom door.

All he wanted...all he needed to do was take a quick peek at her to assure himself she was okay. The door creaked slightly as he opened it, but thankfully, the noise didn't awaken her.

She slept on her back with her dark hair fanned out around her head on the pillow. She looked utterly beautiful, yet fragile with the shoulder bandage visible beneath the spaghetti strap of her red nightgown.

His chest swelled and his stomach muscles tightened in silent rage as he thought of the terror she must have felt...the pain she would continue to feel from the gunshot wound.

The man they sought had to be a cold-blooded monster. Beau couldn't help but wonder who else the man had murdered. He prayed that they would be able to identify him and get him off the streets forever. The monster belonged in a jail cell for what he had done to Lacy, but he belonged in the very depths of hell for what he had done to Peyton.

He closed the bedroom door and went back into the living room, where he sank down on the sofa. The main thing he wanted to do was take care of Peyton for the next couple of days. He had no idea what she might want or need, but whatever it was, he would move heaven and earth to get it for her.

She'd taken a bullet for him. The full impact of what had happened seemed to be hitting him right now. He felt sick knowing that he was responsible for that bullet. He would always carry a huge amount of guilt knowing that he was the cause of her pain.

Once she was awake, he'd turn on his gas-powered generator that not only gave him electricity when he needed it, but also pumped water into the outdoor shower located on the back porch. Although she might not be ready for a shower today, and that was just fine.

During the evenings since he'd been back here and after he left Peyton each day, he'd worked on trying to update the cabin as much as his limited money would allow.

His father hadn't cared about having electricity or any other of the simple amenities. He'd been blacked-out drunk most of the time and when he wasn't passed out, he was on the hunt to get enough money to buy the booze to get blacked-out drunk again.

Beau wasn't sure how long he'd been seated on the sofa and lost in his own thoughts when the bedroom door creaked open and Peyton walked out. She wore a lightweight red robe that matched her nightgown beneath. Her hair was tousled around her head and she would have looked utterly gorgeous if not for the draw of pain that darkened her eyes and tensed her features.

He jumped up from the sofa. "I'd say good morning but by the look on your face, not so much. Sit, and I'll get you your medication."

"Thanks. I'm not sure how it's possible, but my shoulder hurts more now than it did last night," she replied as she sank down on the sofa.

"That's what they often say about any kind of wounds…that the worse day is always the second or third day." He shook out the pills and carried them to her with a glass of water.

She took them and then cast him a wan smile. "Thanks again, Beau. For taking good care of me."

"There's nobody else I'd rather be taking care of," he replied. "As for the *good care*, that remains to be seen since you just woke up."

She released a deep sigh and looked around. "It's nice to be here. This was the one place in my whole life where I always felt safe."

"I'm glad you feel that way," he replied. "Now, how about some breakfast? You need to eat something and I've got some bacon and eggs with your name on them."

"Oh, Beau, I don't want you to go to that kind of trouble for me," she protested.

"It's no trouble at all." He moved back to the icebox and pulled out a pound of bacon and a dozen eggs. "I hope you like scrambled because no matter how hard I try to make different kinds of eggs, they somehow always turn out scrambled."

She laughed and then groaned. "Oh, please don't make me laugh."

"I didn't know I said anything funny," he replied in confusion.

"It's just the fact that the Beau Boudreau, who does everything so well, is beaten by a fried egg."

He flashed her a quick grin and then got busy placing bacon strips into the skillet to fry. "Once we're finished eating, I'll douse the fire."

"Right now the warmth feels good," she said.

"It always feels good in the mornings, but before long it will become way too warm in here."

Within thirty minutes they were seated at the little table in the kitchen area and eating breakfast. "Do you have your copy of the list of men's names we drew up?" she asked.

"I do, but we aren't going to talk about any business today. You need to stay calm and unstressed in order to heal," he replied. "So today you just relax."

She reached for another piece of bacon from the plate in the center of the table. "Then what are we going to talk about today?"

"Oh, I don't know. We used to have a lot of things to talk to each other about." He held her gaze for a long moment.

Her cheeks flushed slightly and then she looked down at her plate. "That was a long time ago, Beau. We were young kids and thought we had our entire futures before us."

"The future for me certainly didn't exactly pan

out the way I intended. But what about you? Has life been good to you, Peyton?"

"There have been good moments and bad moments, but mostly life has been fairly good," she replied.

"You are so beautiful and so smart, why haven't you married before now?" He looked at her curiously. Surely, she'd had plenty of men to choose from over the years.

"I just haven't found the right person I want to spend the rest of my life with yet." She picked at the last of her eggs and then shoved the plate aside.

"What about Sam?" he couldn't help but ask.

"Sam is just a nice man to spend a little time with, but he's not my person. In fact, I broke things off with him the last time we went out."

"You did?" He couldn't help the happiness that filled him at her words.

"I did. It wasn't really fair to keep going out to dinner with him knowing I didn't see a future with him. And now I'm stuffed and I think the pain pill has made me feel a little bit drowsy. Would you mind if I took a short nap?"

"Of course, I wouldn't mind. I want you to rest all you can."

"Then I'll just see you in a little while." She rose from the table and disappeared back into the bedroom.

As he washed the dishes, he wondered if her need for a nap was really an escape from answering anything more about her personal life. He couldn't help but feel good that she'd broken things off with Sam.

However, he couldn't help but wonder if some man in the past had broken her heart. Was that why she hadn't married? He knew she'd been in Shreveport for some time. Maybe she'd had a bad relationship while there, one that had put her off romance altogether? Maybe that was why she had moved back to Black Bayou—because she didn't want to be in a place where her heart had been broken. Of course, he really had no right to know those things about her. He was only speculating about it all.

Still, he couldn't help but wonder if they'd still be together if he hadn't gone to prison. Would their love have lasted through the years? He didn't know the answer, but he'd always believed they would love each other through eternity.

Once the dishes were cleaned up, he took a poker and worked on dousing what was left of the fire. It had already warmed up enough in the shanty that it was no longer needed to take the chill out of the air or cook.

Once the fire was completely out, he stepped outside onto the front porch. Through the thick leaves overhead, the bright sun peeked. Still, this deep in the swamp it was always semi-dark. Of all the things he'd endured in prison, it had definitely taken him some time to adjust to the bright lights of prison.

He was about to turn and go back inside when he heard somebody approaching. All his muscles tensed with fight-or-flight adrenaline. He immediately relaxed as Gator came into view.

"Hey, Beau," Gator said.

"Hi, Gator. Want to come in?" Beau didn't really want any company to disturb Peyton's rest, but in the swamp your door was always open when somebody came visiting. Besides, he owed the old man a big favor for telling him that Peyton had been shot.

"I wouldn't mind coming in to sit a spell," Gator replied.

"Then come on in," Beau said. "But we need to keep our voices down because Peyton is taking a nap."

"Got it," Gator said. He walked in and beelined to the sofa. "So the gossip was true. She got shot?"

"Yes, but thankfully, the bullet only grazed her shoulder. Still, she's in a lot of pain and was traumatized by the whole ordeal."

"No doubt. So you decided to bring her here to heal up?"

"That and to keep her safe from any future harm. Can I get you something to drink?" Beau asked.

"I wouldn't mind a big glass of water," Gator replied as he leaned his walking stick against the coffee table.

Beau got up and poured the old man a glass of water and after handing it to him, he sat in the chair facing Gator. "You think she's still in danger?" Gator asked.

"Not while she's here with me. I think the person who shot her is a town person who wouldn't dare come into the swamp."

"How long do you intend to keep her here?" Gator took a deep swallow of water.

"In a perfect world I'd keep her here until we learn who really killed Lacy, but in reality, I'm just hoping she'll stay for a week or two at the very least."

"You two have been getting into some pretty deep stuff," Gator said. "Personally, I hope you find the bastard who really killed Lacy."

"That's the only way I think Peyton will be truly safe," Beau replied.

"She's important to you," Gator said with a knowing gleam in his eyes.

"She's an old friend and she took a bullet because of me." Beau wasn't about to try to speak about the complexities of his relationship with Peyton any deeper than that.

"An old friend, huh," Gator replied.

At that moment the bedroom door opened and Peyton stepped out. "Oh… I didn't know you had company," she said, obviously embarrassed as she pulled her robe more tightly around her.

"It's all right, Peyton. This is Gator… Gator, this is Peyton LaCroix." Beau got up from the chair and gestured for Peyton to sit.

"It's nice to meet you," Gator said. "I appreciate what you're doing to help Beau." He offered Peyton a toothless grin. "I will say you are mighty easy on the eyes, Ms. Peyton."

"Now, Gator, don't you go flirting with my girl," Beau said, making Gator and Peyton both laugh.

"It's nice to meet you, too," Peyton replied.

"It was Gator who first told me you'd been shot," Beau said.

She looked at Gator in surprise. "How did you know about the shooting?"

"The swamp grapevine. We here in the swamp know most things that go on in town. We sweep your floors and clean your toilets. We're invisible to the people who employ us and meanwhile, we listen and learn. All I did that night was tell Beau what the grapevine was saying about you."

"Well, I sincerely thank you for that," Peyton replied and then shot a warm smile to Beau. "I don't know what I would have done without him."

Her smile created a warmth deep inside Beau. He realized at that moment that what he was really hoping for was that while she was here with him, they could recapture some of the old magic they used to have.

PEYTON HAD BEEN at Beau's for three full days. He'd cooked for her, made sure she took her medicine on time and had done everything he could to take care of her and keep her entertained.

She'd forgotten how funny he could be but as they played cards and various other games to pass the time, he often had her helpless with laughter. She now remembered how much she found his sense of humor sexy and attractive.

He'd also asked her about her time in Shreveport

and what had brought her back to Black Bayou from the big city. She'd told him about her work there and how exhausted she'd become from having no balance in her life. She'd explained to him how she had felt like a hamster running frantically in the wheel with no escape.

He also shared a little bit more about what prison life had been like for him. Her heart had ached as he talked about how those years had been for him.

They had been good, serious conversations, reminiscent of the ones they used to share in the past. She'd worried that they would have nothing to talk about, but they'd also discussed their childhoods... his pain over the fact that his mother had abandoned him and left him to an abusive drunk, and her pain from feeling like her parents had abandoned her at a very young age. They'd opted for a social life where their daughter was merely a hindrance.

Her shoulder had begun to feel better and she'd even managed to take a shower that morning. Now she was ready to get back to what they'd been doing before she'd been shot. She was ready to catch a killer.

Nighttime had fallen and the room was lit with the lanterns. They had just eaten dinner and now Beau sank down on the sofa and she took the chair facing him.

"I think it's time we get back down to business again," she said. "We need to start interviewing the men on our list."

"It's too soon for you to worry about that," he replied. "Maybe by some chance Gravois will identify who shot you and he'll do the work for us."

She gazed at him with narrowed eyes. "Do you really want to leave this all in the hands of Gravois? Beau, a little over a week ago, you were eager to find the killer. And then suddenly you weren't so interested anymore. Something changed with you. Please, Beau, tell me what happened."

He was silent for several long moments and his eyes were as dark as the swamp waters outside. He finally released a deep sigh. "I just came to realize clearing my name isn't that important to me anymore. It won't change the fact that I have absolutely nothing."

"Nothing? What are you talking about, Beau? It will change everything. It will change the way people treat you and how they think about you. And as far as having nothing, you still have your business. Once your name is cleared, I'm sure you'll have a much bigger role there."

"Yeah, about the business…it's not mine."

She frowned at him in confusion. "What are you talking about? Of course it's part yours. The whole thing was your idea…it was your baby from the very beginning."

"Yeah, well, Jack didn't get the memo. When he filled out all the paperwork, he declined to list me as a part owner," he replied, his voice tinged with bitterness. "He told me we'd revisit the issue when I clear my name, but I know nothing is going to change. He wrote me off fifteen years ago and that's that."

"Oh, Beau." She got up from the chair and joined him on the sofa. "That dirtbag stole it from you," she said indignantly. He didn't look at her, but rather stared at some place just over her shoulder. She knew this must have absolutely devastated him. It was a betrayal by a man Beau had considered his very best friend.

She knew Beau had been the driving force for the construction company. Many evenings she and Beau and Jack had sat in this very room and Beau had shared his plans and dreams for the business with Jack. Jack had the money, but Beau had been the brain, the heart and the very soul of the enterprise.

"Beau, look at me," she said softly. Slowly, he met her gaze. "I know how deeply this must have cut you, and I'm sorry. I'm so very sorry." She pulled him awkwardly into her arms for a long hug.

He remained stiff and unyielding for several long moments and then he finally relaxed against her and wrapped his arms around her. He was careful not to touch her shoulder and they remained locked in each other's embrace for a few quiet minutes.

Familiar scents infused her head, the scent of clean male, the faint scent of the cologne he'd always worn and something wild and exciting. It felt good to be held in his arms once again. She realized now she'd never really wanted any other man's arms around her.

She finally raised her head from the crook of his neck and when she gazed at him, her heart seemed to hitch in her throat. His eyes flamed with desire and just that quickly she knew they were going to make love. Not because he wanted her, but rather because she desperately wanted him.

Just one more time she wanted to experience their passion unleashed. It didn't mean she was in love with him. She told herself it didn't have to mean anything. To that end, she leaned forward and placed her lips over his.

He gasped in surprise, but quickly plied her mouth with fiery intent. Their tongues danced together in sweet familiarity, yet also with a new, thrilling excitement.

The kiss lasted until her heart raced uncontrollably and she was half-breathless. Only then did his mouth leave hers, and he trailed a path of nips and kisses down the curve of her jaw and then on down her throat.

Each point of contact shot a shiver of delight up and down her spine. No man had ever made her feel so wild, so completely unbridled, as Beau did even now. His mouth returned to hers and this time his kiss was both feverish and demanding.

She returned the kiss with all the fervor that was inside her. She felt as if she were eighteen years old again and Beau was not only her forever friend, but also her forever lover.

This time the kiss was short-lived. Beau pulled

back from her and his dark eyes glittered wildly in the flickering light from the lantern. "Peyton, we need to stop this," he said, his voice deeper than usual.

"Why? Why do we need to stop, Beau?" she asked.

"Because I can't keep kissing you like this and not want more from you."

His words only heightened her desire for him. "Beau, I want more from you. I want us to make love," she replied.

His eyes flared wide, but he dropped his arms from around her. "We can't do that. You're still hurt and you obviously aren't thinking straight in this moment."

"Beau Boudreau, you've spent the last couple of weeks trying to seduce me and now that you've succeeded, you're saying no to me?" she asked incredulously. "I'm sure we can make love without hurting my shoulder and trust me. I'm thinking perfectly straight. I want you, Beau… I'll confess I've wanted you ever since the moment you walked back into my office."

He stared at her for another long moment and then he got to his feet, bent down and scooped her up in his arms. He carried her into the bedroom, where he gently placed her in the center of the bed.

While he turned on the lantern on the nightstand, she managed to get out of the tank top she'd worn during the day, leaving her clad in her bra and shorts.

"Are you sure about this?" he asked softly as he remained standing by the side of the bed. "Are you really sure, Peyton?" His gaze searched her features. "Because I can turn around right now and leave the room and we'll just forget about this for now."

"Oh, Beau, I've never been surer of anything in my entire life," she replied. "I want you." She raised her hands and beckoned him toward her. "I've wanted you for the last fifteen years."

Still, he paused by the side of the bed, his eyes glittering darkly.

"Beau? What are you doing?" she asked, suddenly unsure what he was going to do.

"Just give me a couple of moments to look at you," he said, his voice husky with obvious desire.

Peyton had never known how powerful a gaze could be, but as Beau's lingered on her, she felt her body responding. Muscles weakened and her nerves tingled as a sweet heat coiled within her.

"Ah, Peyton, you are so beautiful. I dreamed of this moment with you for the last fifteen years. It was thoughts of you that got me through that dark time."

He leaned over and gently touched her lips with his. Soft and tender, his mouth made love to hers. When he was finished with her lips, he moved to her ear, then down her jawline.

As his mouth caressed her, his fingers worked her bra fastening. Once he'd removed it from her, he then moved down to pull off not only her shorts, but her panties as well. He kissed and licked each inch of skin he exposed, driving her out of her mind with need.

By the time he removed his clothing and joined her on the bed, she was already at a fever pitch. Never had she felt so wonderfully alive. Never had she wanted a man more than she wanted Beau now. However, as he started to position himself above her, she shook her head and gently pushed him to his back.

She wanted to kiss him and to caress him until he was utterly wild with his desire for her. She wanted to hear him moan her name over and over again. She wanted him to never, ever want another woman for the rest of his life.

She began to explore the beauty of his body. Her hands ran across his broad chest, feeling his sleek muscles tighten at her touch. She leaned forward and pressed her lips against his skin. She wanted to smell him, taste him and lose herself completely in him.

"Ah, Peyton," he whispered with a groan.

Still, she continued to kiss and nip down his chest. With a low, deep groan, he rolled her over onto her back, and his fingers moved to the very center of her.

Lightly, they danced over the sensitive skin and she thrust her hips upward to meet him. He applied more pressure and his fingers moved faster...and faster. A fiery tension built up inside her and as it crested and her release shuddered through her, she moaned his name over and over again.

When she was still breathless and gasping, he moved between her hips, hovering above her for a single second before sinking slowly into her.

She wrapped her legs around him as tears sprang

to her eyes. Her tears were a mixture of enormous happiness and also a touch of grief…the grief of what might have been and might never be again.

His heart beat the same frantic rhythm as her own as he began to move in and out of her. Slowly at first, he moved in her with a measured pace and created a new, growing tension inside her.

Her breaths quickened as he pumped faster and faster into her. She gasped his name as she spiraled completely out of control and a second powerful climax overtook her.

She gasped his name over and over once again. Then he groaned her name with his own release and together they collapsed side by side as they waited for their breathing to slow to a more normal pace.

Still, Peyton's heart continued to beat an erratic rhythm as she realized the truth of the situation— and the truth was she was still deeply in love with Beau Boudreau.

Chapter Ten

Peyton fell asleep in his arms, but Beau remained wide-awake, listening to her soft breathing and loving the feel of her so intimately close to him. When he'd first arrived back home and reconnected with her, he'd believed all he wanted to do was get Peyton back into his bed. On some level he'd thought that having her once more would get her finally and forever out of his blood.

However, that hadn't happened. He now realized that he was still deeply in love with the young woman he'd once led out of the darkness of the swamp as a child. And he had fallen in love all over again with the woman she'd become.

But he wasn't a lovesick fool. He wasn't blind to reality, and the reality was he was a swamp rat ex-con who had no idea what his future held. Peyton came from a prestigious family. He was sure she was well respected in town; at least she had been before he had gotten involved in her life again.

No, he was no fool. No matter how much he loved

her, there was no future for a swamp rat ex-con without a job and a bright and beautiful, respected defense attorney.

His only goal now was to keep her safe from harm. Once he knew she was no longer in danger, he'd disappear from her life once and for all. It was the best thing he could do for her...because he loved her enough to let her go.

He finally fell asleep and into nightmares of Peyton running through the swamp with the Honey Island Swamp Monster chasing after her. Beau raced after them, running as fast as he could in his desperation to get to her before the monster caught her.

Her terrified screams filled the air, echoing through the thick brush and trees and shooting terror through his veins. The swamp, which had always been his friend, now fought against him. Tree limbs reached out to slow him down and thick tubers tried to trip him up.

Spanish moss swept across his face, momentarily blinding him again and again. Her screams now came from farther and farther away and he yelled her name, horrified that he was going to lose her to the monster.

He came awake with a deep gasp and shot straight up in the bed. For a moment he was disoriented as his heart beat a thousand beats a minute, and his breathing was hard and labored.

Thankfully, the lantern was still lit on the nightstand. He gazed next to him where Peyton remained sleeping soundly. Thankfully, he hadn't woken her. He released a shuddery sigh of relief.

It had all just been a nightmare. He rubbed his hands up and down his face. Thank God it had just been a very bad dream. He remained sitting for several minutes and then slid out of the bed. His internal alarm clock let him know it was nearly morning.

Bending down, he grabbed the jeans and boxers he'd worn the day before and then carried them out of the bedroom. He pulled them on in the living room and then stepped out the front door in an effort to completely shrug off the last vestiges of the horrible dream.

It was still dark out, but he could feel the swamp breathing all around him. Morning birds sang from the treetops, and small animals rustled in the brush. He took several deep breaths of the humid air, the myriad scents mingling together to smell like home.

The swamp might have been his enemy in his nightmares, but in truth it was his family and his friend. It was where he belonged, just like Peyton belonged in town. However, before she could return to her own life, he had to catch a killer. Once he caught the guilty party then Peyton would be safe, and his name would be cleared.

Peyton. Making love to her again had been as wonderful…as earth-shattering…as he remembered. If anything, it had been even better than he remembered. He'd made love to her before when she was a young, innocent woman, but last night she'd been a mature woman who had matched him in his fervor, in his very hunger to intimately connect with her.

With a heavy sigh, he turned and went back inside. It was too warm this morning to make a fire, so breakfast would be croissants and sweet rolls and juice.

Eventually, he wanted to buy a small oven and refrigerator that he could run on the generator, but he didn't have the funds to do anything else to further modernize the place. He also still had no idea now how he was going to make future funds, so he needed to hang on to what he had left.

The idea of crawling back to Jack to ask for a job in the company Beau thought had been part his stuck in his craw. Eventually, he'd figure something out for himself. If nothing else, Beau was a survivor.

It was about an hour later when Peyton came out of the bedroom. She was clad only in her nightgown and robe and shot him a radiant smile. "Good morning," she said. She waltzed over to him and kissed him soundly on the cheek.

"Whoa, somebody is in a good mood this morning," he replied as she walked over to the sofa and sank down. Her gaze was warm and open and without any defensive shutters to keep him out.

"I'm in a great mood, and why shouldn't I be? My shoulder has pretty much stopped hurting, a handsome hunk of a man made sweet love to me last night and I slept like a baby."

He couldn't look at her any longer. He couldn't

stand to see the joyous look in her eyes. He definitely didn't want to talk about what they'd shared the night before. "I didn't light a fire this morning. It's already warm in here, so I figured we could just have juice and croissants for breakfast."

"That's fine with me," she replied, her voice more subdued than it had been moments before.

He got busy plating the croissants and sweet rolls, grabbed a couple of paper towels to use for napkins and carried it all to the coffee table. He then poured two glasses of juice and joined her on the sofa.

For a couple of minutes they ate in silence. Rather than being a comfortable quiet, it was strained and tense. "Well, are we going to talk about the elephant in the room or are we going to just pretend it didn't happen?" she finally asked. Her gaze held his searchingly. "I definitely smell regret in the room."

He stifled a deep sigh. "*Ma chérie*, how could I ever regret making love to you? It was beyond wonderful to have you in my arms once again."

"It was beyond wonderful to be in your arms again," she replied, some of her tense energy dissipating. "And now that I've had breakfast, if you don't mind, I'd like to take a shower."

"No problem," Beau said with an inward sigh of relief. "I'll go start the pump." Apparently, all she'd needed was the affirmation that last night had been wonderful for both of them. He'd been afraid she'd want to talk about a future, and he wasn't ready yet to tell her there was no future for them.

Last night had been beyond wonderful, but it was a one-time thing and it would never happen again. He didn't want to lead her on by making love with her again.

Thirty minutes later she was in the enclosed shower on the back porch and visions of her naked and beneath the spray of water played over and over in his head. *Mon Dieu*, even though he was determined not to be with her again, that didn't stop the raw desire for her that roared through him.

She was in the shower for about fifteen minutes before she raced from the back porch to the bedroom clad only in a towel. Finally, she came back into the living room dressed in a red tank top and a pair of navy blue shorts. She looked refreshed and better than she had in days.

She sank down on the sofa next to him. "It's time for us to get back to work," she said. "I'm feeling fine now and I'm more determined than ever to find the man who killed Lacy and shot me."

"Peyton, I don't want you involved in this anymore," Beau said firmly.

"Well, tough, I *am* involved, and I intend to stay involved," she replied just as firmly. "Now, can I see your copy of the list we made up from the initials? We need to come up with a game plan."

"I just don't think it's a good idea for you to be a part of this anymore," he replied, not moving from his seat on the sofa. "You need to distance yourself from the investigation. It might help keep you safe."

"And it might not." She stared at him for a long moment. "Beau, I can either do this with you or I can do it all alone, but one way or another I'm moving forward with the investigation."

He knew she was telling the truth, and there was no way he intended to allow her to move forward by herself. Reluctantly, he got up, walked to the little desk by the door and then opened the drawer that held the paperwork.

He returned to the sofa and handed it to her. She then spread it out on the top of the coffee table. She stared down at the list of names and then released a deep sigh. "Now that I've had a few days away from this, I realize our initial plan to interview these men is pretty impractical. First of all, it's going to take us forever to speak to each person and secondly, I don't think the killer is suddenly going to just confess to us because we asked him a few questions."

He frowned at her. "Then how are we going to move forward?"

A frown creased her forehead as well. "It would help if Gravois would interview all these men and give the whole thing a real air of legitimacy," she said in obvious frustration. "He's better trained in interviewing suspects than we are. He might be able to see subtle signs of deception."

"I seriously doubt that, but in any case, we both know Gravois isn't going to lift a single finger to help us out," he replied with his own disgust. Beau expected absolutely nothing from the chief of police. In truth, he wished Gravois would solve the deaths of the young women from the swamp who were supposed to be victims of the Honey Island Swamp Monster.

In the meantime, he and Peyton needed to come up with a plan to catch their own killer and at the moment he had no idea what that might be. They sat stewing in their own thoughts for several long moments.

"I think I've got it," she suddenly said and sat up straighter. Her eyes began to sparkle with the bright light that Beau always loved to see, and a swift new dart of desire pierced through him.

"What?" He tried to focus on what she said and not how the scent of her stirred his senses or how her body heat wafted over him. He mentally shook himself. "Do you have a new plan?" he asked.

"I think I do." A frown of concentration creased her forehead once again as she stared down at the list. "What if we send letters to all the men on the list? The letters would say something like, 'I saw you kill Lacy Dupree. Meet me at such-and-such a place and bring lots of cash to keep my mouth shut forever.'"

She looked back up at him. "If you were an innocent man, would you respond to that note? Would you go to the place to meet a blackmailer?"

He thought for a long moment. "No, I'd probably just toss the letter away and think some kook sent it." He continued to think about the new plan and then he smiled at her. "This just might work," he said as an edge of excitement filled him. "I think the killer would definitely show up."

"We've got nothing to lose by trying this, right?"

"Right," he replied. "At this point we have absolutely nothing to lose."

"Then we need to go to my office. I've got the list of addresses there from the tax records. We can match the addresses with names and then write up the letter and I can make copies. I'll call Kylie to come in and help us address and stamp the envelopes and then we can get them into the mail by the end of the day."

She leaned forward and wrapped her arms around his neck. "I feel it in my heart, Beau. We're going to catch this person, and your name will finally be cleared."

Her voice was a soft whisper against his neck and evoked in him a renewed wild desire to take her into the bedroom and make love to her all over again.

He quickly stood, breaking the embrace that threatened to undo his conviction to never make love to her again. "Then let's get ready to go."

"Give me fifteen minutes or so and I'll be ready," she replied. She got up and headed into the bedroom.

He breathed a sigh of relief as his desire slowly dissipated. Instead, he thought about the plan she'd come up with. Could it work?

Would the killer really respond to the letter and show up at a specific place and time to pay off a blackmailer? Would any innocent men show up out of sheer curiosity? He couldn't imagine anyone doing that, but he supposed it might be possible.

Still, in any case, this might narrow the field to only a few men—and one of them would surely be Lacy's killer, the man who had framed him and shot Peyton.

God, he wanted the answer to the question that had haunted him for the past fifteen years. Who had killed Lacy Dupree? When he'd lost his necklace, he'd never dreamed somebody would find it and use it to frame him for murder. He'd never dreamed that he'd be locked up in prison for fifteen long years.

An hour later they were in Peyton's office. She sat in her chair behind her desk and he pulled the other chair around to sit right next to her. They began working on matching all the names to the addresses. Thankfully, they had viable addresses for all of them.

They next moved on to crafting the details of the letter. "Where is a good place for us to set up this meet?" she asked.

Beau frowned thoughtfully. "It has to be someplace fairly isolated and yet you and I need places to hide so the perp doesn't initially see us. There also needs to be enough light that we can see who exactly he is."

"Any ideas?" she asked.

"I'm thinking. What time do you think this meeting should take place?" he asked.

She frowned. "I don't know… I was thinking around midnight—what do you think?"

He shrugged. "Midnight sounds fine with me, and how about Vincent's Grocery? The place has security lights all around it and if we tell the man to meet us on the south side, then you and I could step into the cover of the swamp to watch who shows up."

"That sounds perfect," she replied. "What day do we want to make it? The letters should reach everyone by day after tomorrow at the latest."

"Then let's make the meet for Friday night," Beau replied. That was four days from now. He had a feeling they were going to be the longest days of his and Peyton's lives.

The sound of the outside door opening shot Beau up and out of his chair. He took only a couple of steps and then relaxed as Kylie came into the inner office.

"Oh, boss, I'm so glad to see you," the young woman said as Beau returned to his chair. "How are you feeling? You look really good. Beau must be taking good care of you."

Peyton shot him a warm smile. "He has definitely been taking good care of me."

"She's been an easy patient," Beau said.

"That's good to hear. And you're really doing okay?"

"I promise. I'm doing just fine," Peyton assured her.

"I just can't believe you were shot," Kylie replied.

"Well, I was, and I lived to tell the tale." Peyton smiled at the young woman.

"You said on the phone that you have some envelopes for me to address?" Kylie asked.

"Yes, here's the list of names and addresses, and we want to use the plain envelopes, not my official ones," Peyton instructed. "And wear gloves so no fingerprints are on them."

Kylie took the list from her. "Got it. I'll get right to it." She left the inner office.

"She seems like a good kid," Beau said once she was gone.

"She is, and there are days I wouldn't know what to do without her. She's very bright and a hard worker," Peyton replied. "Now, let's get back to work on this letter."

It took them a half an hour to complete the letter, after which Peyton made all the copies. By that time Kylie had all the envelopes addressed.

"Kylie, I don't know for sure when our usual office hours will resume, but I'd appreciate it if you continue monitoring the front desk during the day in case somebody needs my representation," Peyton said. "However if you don't feel safe doing that, then we'll just lock the place up for the time being."

"I'm not afraid. I'll be here every day. You can depend on me to hold down the fort while you're gone," Kylie replied. She gestured to the stack of envelopes. "I don't know what the two of you are up to, but I hope it works out the way you want it to."

"So do we," Beau replied.

Beau and Peyton had made the decision not to allow Kylie to see the letters or share with her what they were doing. "Thanks, Kylie. You can go ahead and take off now," Peyton said.

It took them another half hour after Kylie left to stuff and stamp the envelopes. They both wore gloves as well. He was surprised to realize darkness had fallen outside. The project had taken far longer than he'd expected and the hours had flown by.

Peyton placed the envelopes in her purse and then they left the building. Besides the actual post office building, there were three public mail drop boxes around town.

They agreed to divide the letters and drop some into all three. Once it was done, they were both silent on the way back to the swamp.

When they reached Beau's place, Peyton collapsed on the sofa and released a deep sigh. He sank down next to her, the enormity of what they'd just put into place whirling around in his head.

"How are you feeling?" he asked her.

"Nervous…anxious and a little bit excited," she replied. "What about you?"

"Nervous…anxious and a little bit excited," he said, making her laugh.

Her eyes shimmered as she moved closer to him. "Oh, Beau, just think, in a matter of four days it could finally all be over." She moved even closer to him and he couldn't help but draw her into his embrace.

He closed his eyes as he held her, breathing in her unique scent and remembering every moment of their lovemaking. He thought of each moment of laughter they had shared over the past few days and his heart squeezed tight. Four more days and the real murderer would be exposed. Four more days and his name would be cleared of the murder that had sent him away.

He should be deliriously happy that it was all coming to an end. However, in this moment with Peyton in his arms, all he could think about was how in four more days it would be time for Beau to get out of Peyton's life for good.

PEYTON PACED THE small confines of the shanty while Beau sat on the sofa watching her. Two days had passed since they'd sent out the letters. By now the killer had probably received his. Two more nights and hopefully, they would meet the killer face-to-face.

That thought had her filled with a wild energy. This had to work. Their little scheme had to uncover the man who had killed Lacy and framed Beau. If this didn't work, she wouldn't know how to move forward on the case.

For the past two nights Beau had slept in the bed with her, but he hadn't made any move to make love to her again. Despite her yearning for him, she hadn't pressed him on the issue.

However, she did yearn for him. She wanted to feel his lips on hers, taste his desire on his mouth again. She desperately wanted to feel his naked body move against hers as he possessed her completely once again.

They had eaten dinner a little while ago and bed-
time would soon be approaching. Maybe he had been
hesitant to make love to her again. Maybe he didn't
realize the depth of her feelings where he was concerned. Or perhaps it was just the stress and anxiety about how things were going to go down on
Friday night.

"Would you please stop the pacing," he now said,
his voice a bit terse. "You're making me more stressed
out."

She walked over to the sofa and sank down next
to him. "With each minute that passes I get more
stressed and more anxious for Friday night to be
over with."

"I feel the same way," he admitted. "The hours
can't go by fast enough. I keep twisting and turning
different scenarios in my head, trying to think of
ways this plan could fail."

"It's not going to fail," she replied firmly. "It can't
fail."

She smiled at him. He looked so hot in a pair of
worn jeans and a white T-shirt. His dark, shiny hair
had grown slightly shaggy over the past couple of
weeks, making him look more like the young man
she'd fallen so deeply in love with, the man she was
still so deeply in love with.

"It's going to be wonderful to finally know who
framed you for the murder," she said.

"I definitely want to know the answer," he replied
with a touch of anger in his voice. "I want to know

who stole my life away from me. The bastard stole everything good from me. I also want to know who attacked and shot you."

She placed a hand on his arm. "Two more days and we'll have all the answers."

"I hope so."

She leaned closer to him. "And then we'll have to plan to do something wonderful to celebrate our success," she said.

"I don't think I'll be in the mood for much of a celebration," he replied with a frown.

She cuddled even closer against him. "Surely, we could figure out something to do to celebrate," she said in what she hoped was a seductive voice. "Maybe we could start our celebration right here and right now."

To her surprise, he gently pushed away from her and stood. "I think I'll go start the generator so we can charge up our phones."

She frowned as she watched him walk through the kitchen area and then disappear out the back door. Normally, Beau would be the one trying to seduce her back into his bed, but now she found herself trying to seduce him.

Had she somehow disappointed him when they'd made love before? He certainly hadn't acted disappointed in any way during the act. So why wasn't he rushing to take her to bed and make love with her again?

She'd believed they were rebuilding a relationship, a love that had been denied to them by a terrible fate. She could have sworn he was falling back in love with her as she was with him.

Had she been wrong all along? Had his sole purpose been to use her to help him find the killer? To simply have her in his bed one more time for old time's sake? God, she hoped that wasn't the case. The very idea of that being true absolutely crushed her.

The thrum of the generator filled the room. She got up from the sofa and went into Beau's bedroom to grab her cell phone and cord. The one working outlet was in the kitchen. As she plugged in, Beau came back inside.

He went into the bedroom and returned a moment later with his phone. Once he had his plugged in, he sank down in the chair and she returned to the sofa.

"We'll let them charge but sooner or later I need to run to Vincent's and get more gasoline."

She knew the little grocery store had a single gas pump on one side of the building. "Do you want me to go with you when you go?"

"No, that's not necessary. You should be safe here for me to make a quick run," he replied. His voice held a distance and his eyes were shuttered closed.

Now that she thought about it, he'd been fairly distant with her all day long. Was it just because of the stress of the case coming to an end? She would have thought that would make him deliriously happy but while he mouthed the words, she didn't feel any real happiness radiating from him.

Suddenly, her love for him felt too enormous to hold inside. She wanted his name cleared, but more than that she wanted a future with him. She wanted to fulfill the dreams they had once made, dreams of loving each other forever and her having his babies.

Fate had given them a second chance to make those dreams come true—all he had to do was love her like he had years before. She'd really thought she'd felt that emanating from him over the past couple of weeks, but maybe she'd been wrong. Or perhaps all she had to do was tell him how deeply she'd fallen in love with him again… Maybe he just needed to hear her words of love.

"Beau, can we have a serious conversation?" she asked.

"Of course. What's up? Are you suddenly having second thoughts about our plan?" He gazed at her curiously.

"No, nothing like that," she replied. She gazed at him for a long moment, suddenly feeling shy and uncertain. She had no idea how he might react, but the one thing she was certain of was her love for him.

"I just wanted you to know that I'm wildly and desperately in love with you." The words blurted out of her before she even knew for sure how she intended to tell him her feelings.

He appeared to look at her in stunned surprise. Initially, she thought she saw a flash of wild joy in the depths of his eyes but then they once again shuttered darkly against her. "I'm not surprised you think you're in love with me. After all, I took care of you when you were in pain and I'm now doing the best that I can to guard your life."

"Beau, I don't just *think* I'm in love with you. I know I am." She got up from the sofa and crouched in front of where he sat in the chair. "I loved you when I was a young girl, and now I love you with the maturity of the woman I've become. I want to spend the rest of my life with you. I want to have your babies. Beau, I want the future we once promised to each other. After Friday night we can finally have it all... We can have all our dreams come true."

His muscles bunched and the knot in his jaw began to tick. "That future was destroyed."

"But it doesn't have to be destroyed," she protested. "It was just postponed for fifteen years. We can still have it all, Beau. We catch the bad guy and clear your name and then the future is ours."

The knot in his jaw clenched and unclenched. "And what kind of future do you really think you're going to have with me?" He got up from the chair, and to her surprise he half knocked her over as he stood and took several steps away from her. He turned back to look at her and his eyes blazed with emotions she couldn't begin to decipher.

"Tell me what you foresee when you think about a future with me," he said. "Have you considered the fact that I'm an ex-con swamp rat without a job? Have you thought about the fact that I don't even know what I'm going to do when this is all over? I'm trash, Peyton, and you deserve much better."

"Don't say that," she replied and she quickly scrambled back to her feet. "You are not trash, Beau Boudreau. And you are not a swamp rat. I'm not worried about you not having a job. You're smart and resourceful, and there's no doubt in my mind that you'll figure something out."

He raked a hand through his hair and gazed at some point over her head. "It's not going to work, Peyton," he said.

She took several steps closer to him. "As long as we love each other, we'll make it work. Look at me, Beau. Look at me and tell me you don't love me."

His gaze met hers. "It doesn't matter whether I love you or not." The muscle in his jaw ticked faster. "The truth of the matter is I'm not sure I can ever forgive you."

"Forgive me?" She looked at him in stunned confusion. "Forgive me for what?"

His entire body tensed and there was no mistaking the anger that suddenly emanated from him. "You knew me better than anyone else in the world, Peyton. You knew all there was to know about me, and yet you didn't believe in me."

"Beau, I'm sorry, but after you were convicted, I'll admit I didn't know what to believe," she admitted.

"I'm talking about before that. I'm talking about the minute you heard that I'd been arrested for the murder. You didn't come down to the jail and talk to me. You didn't come to hear what I had to say. I waited and waited in that jail cell for my girl to come and offer me support." His features appeared tortured with a combination of grief and anger.

She stepped toward him and reached out in an effort to touch him, to somehow soothe him. She'd never dreamed he had these kinds of feelings toward her. She'd never realized what a betrayal that had been to him.

He took several steps backward from her. "I needed you, Peyton, but you never came. When it came right down to it, you believed what everyone else believed about me...that I was a cheat and a coldhearted killer." He released a bitter laugh. "And what a stupid murderer I was...to leave my necklace wrapped around Lacy's neck and lead the police right to me. Still, you abandoned me when I needed you most."

Tears sprang to her eyes. "I'm sorry. Beau, I was eighteen years old. When I heard you'd been arrested, I didn't know what to do. I had everyone talking to me...confusing me. I was so young, Beau. I didn't know how to handle what was happening."

Hot tears ran down her cheeks as she realized the depth of his pain. She took several steps toward him, wanting to touch him, to embrace him in an effort to somehow heal this...heal him. "I'm sorry, Beau. I'm so sorry I let you down. In my heart of hearts, I never believed you were guilty. Please forgive me for not being there for you."

He'd apparently held in these feelings about her

for the past fifteen years, and she didn't know how to fix this except to plead for his forgiveness. "Beau, please… I love you so much. Please, tell me we can get past this and that you love me, too."

The anger left his features, leaving behind a weary exhaustion. "I'm going to go get some gas. I definitely need some fresh air." He didn't wait for a response, but rather turned on his heel, grabbed his cell phone from the desk and then strode out the front door.

Chapter Eleven

Thick emotion pressed tight against Beau's chest as he shut off the generator and then grabbed the two plastic gas containers off the back porch. He then headed away from the shanty.

He hadn't meant to go there with her. He'd never intended to tell her how badly he'd felt betrayed by her all those years ago. But it had been the best defense against her words of love. Holding that against her would give him a reason to tell her they'd never have a future together.

Now her words of love played and replayed in his head. He'd wanted her to fall back in love with him; he'd wanted her to love him as much as he loved her. But he'd recognized the truth, and the truth of the matter was in this case love just wasn't enough.

He couldn't change who he was...what he was. No matter how much they loved each other, he still had no viable future to offer her. She was far better off without him.

Tears blurred his vision as he walked through the

dark paths toward the grocery store. She loved him, and his heart should be singing with happiness.

The moment he'd found out she was still single, and then when he'd walked into her office and seen her again, his heart had remembered all the wonderful things about her...all the magical moments they had shared together. He'd told himself all he wanted was to get her into his bed, but he'd been lying to himself. He'd wanted her for an eternity.

He'd been a damn fool. He'd not only fooled himself into thinking they could pick up where they'd left off all those years ago, but he'd also toyed with her emotions by allowing her to believe the same thing.

He now needed to embrace all the anger he'd felt when she hadn't come to talk to him, when she hadn't shown her support to him after he'd been arrested. He had to make his anger keep a strong shield around his heart. He needed that shield to keep her out of his life. It was the kindest thing he could do for her.

She would be fine without him. She was smart and beautiful and eventually, she'd find a man worthy of her love. And they would build a wonderful life together.

She had a respectable business to build and Beau would only be a liability in her life. He had to make her see that the dreams they'd had fifteen years ago simply weren't viable in the real world. They had merely been the innocent fantasies of children.

"Yo, Beau." Gator appeared on the path in front of him.

"Hey, Gator," Beau replied. He quickly swallowed hard against all his emotions. The very last thing he wanted was for Gator to see him distraught or teary-eyed.

"I've never known you to make so much noise traveling through the swamp, but just now you definitely sounded like a pissed-off boar crashing around," Gator said.

Beau held up the two gas cans. "I probably was crashing around. I'm just heading to Vincent's to get some gas for my generator."

"How's that pretty woman of yours doing?" Gator asked.

"She's pretty much healed up so she's doing just fine," Beau replied. He wanted to insist to Gator that Peyton wasn't his woman, but he couldn't force the words to his lips right now.

"Any word from Gravois on who shot her?"

"No, nothing. And I'm assuming there's been no break in the swamp women's murders."

"Nothing that I've heard, and you know I hear most things," Gator replied.

"I've never known a man who has murders happening right under his nose and can't catch the guilty person," Beau said in disgust.

"He put you behind bars quick enough," Gator said.

"You got that right. He can solve a crime wrongly if there's a convenient swamp rat to take the fall."

"That's probably what's going to happen with the

murders that have taken place. He'll find somebody from the swamp to lock up, but the murders will continue 'cause he'll lock up the wrong person."

"So you think it's a townie killing those women?" Beau asked.

"My gut says so, and my gut usually isn't wrong."

"You probably have that right," Beau replied. "By the way, what are you doing sneaking around out here?"

Gator laughed. "You know I sometimes like sneaking around. I get tired of the four walls and feel the need to be out here in the wild. You know how it is, Beau."

"I do, and now I'd better get moving. I don't want to leave Peyton alone for too long," Beau replied.

"Go on, then," Gator said. "I'll see you later."

Beau continued forward as Gator disappeared into the darkness. At least meeting the old man had forced Beau to pull himself together.

Now all he felt was a deep, burning sadness in knowing that after Friday night he would say goodbye to Peyton forever.

THE MINUTE BEAU LEFT, Peyton collapsed in tears on the sofa. She'd truly believed she and Beau had been working toward a future together. She'd truly believed he was as deeply in love with her as she was with him. And maybe he was…but he couldn't forgive her.

She'd never dreamed that he'd been holding in so much resentment toward her. She didn't know how to fix this. She didn't know how to make right a mistake she'd made fifteen years ago.

At that time, she'd been so young. Her parents had hammered into her Beau's guilt, as had her girlfriends, especially when she'd learned that Beau had been in Lacy's room that night. She'd been confused and hadn't known what to do so in the end, she'd done nothing. And that had been her mistake…her sin.

There was no way to make Beau understand. There was a part of her that didn't understand why she hadn't run to Beau to hear his side of the story, why she hadn't been there to support him through the ordeal. Definitely, her youth had played into it.

She'd only been eighteen years old, and fairly sheltered at that. She hadn't known anything about crime and what happened when a person was arrested. She hadn't even known she could go to the jail and speak with Beau.

And the payment for that one mistake was that she would never truly have Beau's love again. There would be no future for them as long as he held on to that resentment.

Her grief stabbed straight into her heart, hurting with an agonizing pain she'd never felt before. It was more painful than the day she'd lost him to prison, more painful than a bullet in the shoulder.

Over the past couple of weeks, she'd seen Beau and the man that he had become. She'd actually envisioned building a life with him, building a family with him. She saw them reclaiming the dreams and plans they had made as a young couple in love. But apparently, that wasn't going to happen now.

She'd cried over the demise of those dreams on the day he'd been convicted and sent to prison, and she now cried over the death of them once again.

She had to face reality, and the reality was that apparently, he didn't love her after all. She would've sworn that she'd seen his love for her shining in his eyes. She'd believed she'd felt his love for her in his simplest touch. How had she been so wrong about things? And why hadn't he told her how much he resented her from the very beginning?

She didn't know how long she cried before she finally sat up and wiped her tears away. Maybe she could talk to him again when he came back from getting the gas. There had to be a way for her to make him forgive her. There just had to be a way that they could get beyond this and finally live the future they'd once dreamed about.

She got off the sofa and went to the icebox. She pulled out of it a cold bottle of water. She ran the bottle across her forehead where a headache threatened to blossom, then she opened it and took several drinks. She carried it back to the sofa, where she sank back down and placed the bottle on the coffee table.

Footsteps sounded outside the shanty, and she got up from the sofa and quickly wiped the last of her tears off her cheeks. She drew several deep breaths and prepared herself to beg for Beau's forgiveness…

to beg him for his love again. When it came to this, she had no pride. She would beg and plead to get him to forgive her.

A quick knock sounded and then the door opened. Jack Fontenot walked in. "Peyton," he said, sounding surprised. "I didn't expect to see you here."

"Jack," she replied with equal surprise. "Beau's not here right now. He went down to Vincent's to get gas for the generator."

"Actually, I knew Beau wasn't here and I knew you were here. It's actually you I wanted to talk to."

"Me? What do you want to talk to me about?" she asked. And how did he know that Beau wasn't here? An edge of disquiet suddenly swept through her.

"I wanted to talk to you about your investigation into Lacy's murder," he said.

"Okay. Why don't you have a seat." She gestured toward the sofa.

"Thanks, but I'll just stand. I don't intend to be here that long," he replied. "I was just wondering how close you and Beau are to naming the guilty party?"

"Very close," she replied.

"And are you keeping close contact with Gravois about the murderer?" he asked.

"Gravois hasn't been very interested in our investigation," she admitted. "Jack, you should probably come back when Beau is here."

"I told you I don't need to talk to Beau. Aren't you listening to me?" Jack's blue eyes appeared as cold as ice as he took another step toward her.

Her Spidey senses went on high alert and all her muscles tensed. The scent of danger suddenly filled the room and half dizzied her mind. "Well, I'd feel more comfortable to speak to you with Beau here. So I think it's time for you to go, Jack," she said stiffly. She walked around him and toward the front door.

"I can't go until I confess all my sins to you."

"Your sins?" She looked at him in confusion.

"I tried to warn you off the case, Peyton. When I attacked you by your car, I warned you to drop your investigation, but you didn't listen to me," he said.

She gasped. *Jack?* It had been Jack who'd shoved her against her car and smashed her in the face? "You did that to me? But why? Why on earth would you care what we were doing?" And then it hit her. Of course he cared. He cared because he had killed Lacy. Beau's best friend had killed Lacy and framed Beau.

"Bingo," Jack said. "I can see by the look on your face that you get it now." His features twisted into a frightening mask of anger. "That little bitch wanted me to pay her off to keep her mouth shut about all the times I visited her and what we did while I was with her."

His voice rose as he continued, "She wanted me to go to my parents and get fifty thousand dollars. She threatened to destroy my reputation at a time when we were going forward with the construction company. I'd found Beau's necklace that day at a job we had done and it seemed like the perfect opportunity to kill two birds with one stone. I knew the construction business would be successful, so why share it with anyone?"

"Jack, my God, he was your best friend," Peyton replied, stunned by what the man had just told her and also now terrified about her own safety. They'd considered Jack, but had quickly taken him off their list of potential suspects. He hadn't even received one of their letters.

"Friends come and go, but a successful business and money are what counts in life. Now all I need to do is take care of you, and Beau will be too heartbroken to care about who killed Lacy. He'll drop the investigation in his grief over you."

He pulled from the back of his jeans a handheld three-prong gardening cultivator. "I'll make sure I rip out your throat so Gravois thinks it's the same killer who has been murdering swamp women."

For a brief moment Peyton remained frozen in place, her brain swirling around in an attempt to make sense of things. There was madness in the air...utter madness and death. Then Jack lunged at her. With a scream, she whirled around and ran out the front door.

She raced down the walkway with Jack's footsteps thundering just behind her. Thankfully, darkness had fallen. Surely, she could lose him in the dark. Still, Jack had spent a lot of his youth here in the swamp so he wouldn't be afraid to follow her wherever she went.

Beau, where are you? Her heart screamed his

name over and over again. How long before he returned to the cabin? What would he think when he found her gone? Would he come looking for her or would he be relieved that she was no longer there?

All these thoughts raced through her head as she ran for her life. The dark swamp seemed to fight with her as she quickly became disoriented. Branches seemed to grab for her and more than once she tripped and nearly fell. The Spanish moss fluttered across her face over and over again, like a shroud attempting to capture her.

The sound of Jack crashing through the thick vegetation after her filled her with a terror she'd never known. She cried out as she stepped into the swamp water and her foot sank into the muck. She yanked her foot free and continued running.

Her breaths came in panicked, sobbing gasps, causing a painful stitch to stab into her side. He was gaining ground on her. Dear God, he was just behind her and she couldn't run any faster. She was pushing herself as hard as she could. Still, she could hear his panting breaths and imagined she could feel his hot breath on the back of her neck.

Beau. His name now filled her head with the grief of knowing she would never see him again. Jack was going to catch her, and he'd use the gardening tool to rip out her throat. Beau or somebody else would eventually find her dead body and Gravois would write it up as just another Honey Island Swamp Monster attack.

BEAU REACHED VINCENT's and went inside the small store. There was a limited meat counter, several bins full of vegetables and fruits and rows of canned goods and sundry other items.

Vincent was behind the counter. Beau wouldn't even begin to guess the old man's age, but despite his advanced years, Vincent could be found behind the counter almost every single day. Beau knew he was a widower who lived in a small apartment in the back of the business.

Vincent was neither town nor swamp, but rather a hybrid of both, who easily moved back and forth between the two worlds. Still, all the people who lived in the swamp appreciated the store so close to the wild.

"Hey, Vincent," he greeted him.

"Hi, Beau. How's it going?"

"It's going. How are you doing?"

"The arthritis is kicking my butt lately, but other than that I got no complaints," he replied. "Now, what can I do for you tonight?"

"I need ten gallons of gas." Beau got his wallet out to pay for the purchase.

"Okay, you're all set and the pump is on," Vincent said once he got Beau's money.

"Thanks, Vincent." Beau picked up the gas containers, walked back out the front door and then around to the side of the building where the single pump was located.

As he filled first one of the containers and then

the other one, his thoughts returned to Peyton. Somehow, they needed to coexist for two more days and then hopefully the killer would be caught and Peyton could get back to her real life.

Dammit, he shouldn't have allowed his anger to get the best of him. He should have never spoken to her about the resentment that now didn't seem so important in the grand scheme of things. At least, he should have waited until after Friday night to speak to her about it. The last thing he wanted to do was push her out of the shanty before Friday night.

He still had no idea what he intended to do with his future, but he'd eventually figure something out. He just needed time. Once the real killer was caught and Peyton's safety was assured, his brain would be cleared to think about what his next move forward would be.

With both cans filled, he left the grocery store and headed back toward home. The cans were unwieldy enough to keep him at a slow pace as he traversed the small trails that would eventually lead him back to the shanty.

He knew he'd broken Peyton's heart before he'd left. He also knew he was going to have to somehow navigate her emotions so that she'd stay with him for as long as she was in danger.

The next couple of days were probably going to be difficult, but they had to remember that the end goal was to catch a murderer.

He'd only gone a short distance when he first

heard it. A high-pitched scream that echoed through the darkness. He stopped in his tracks, unsure if the scream had been from a person or some sort of a wild animal.

The scream sounded again. This time he knew it was a person. It was Peyton. He dropped the gas cans and ran toward where he thought the shriek had come from.

Adrenaline surged through him. His heart beat a frantic rhythm as he crashed through the thickets. "Peyton!" he cried. What was happening? Why was she screaming? Had she tried to leave and somehow fallen into the swamp water? There was no question she was in some sort of danger. "Peyton!" he yelled again.

"Beau!" Her cry came from someplace to his right. He reached a trail and veered off in that direction. Where was she? Oh, God, it was just like the nightmare he'd had where she'd been chased by the Honey Island Swamp Monster and he'd been unable to find her to save her.

He had to find her now. This wasn't a dream where he would wake up with her safe beside him. He continued to run, slapping at branches and leaves that threatened to slow him down. His heart threatened to beat out of his chest as deep gasps exploded out of him.

She screamed again and this time he was closer to her. Her scream not only sounded terrified, but it was also filled with pain. What was happening to her? He surged ahead, silently praying that when he reached her, she would be all right.

There was a break in the darkness as the overhead vegetation thinned and the full moonlight shone down. That was when he saw them… Peyton was on her back and Jack stood over her with some sort of weapon in his hand.

For a moment Beau couldn't make sense of what he saw. Jack? Why was Jack out here attacking Peyton? But the *why* didn't matter. At the moment the big man didn't see Beau. Beau jumped on his back and took him down to the ground.

Peyton sobbed as she crab-walked backward to get out of the way. Beau glanced at her and realized her lower leg was bleeding badly.

"You bastard, what are you doing?" Beau roared in anger as he slammed his fist into Jack's jaw. He reared backward as Jack swung a gardening tool at Beau's face.

Beau dodged the hit and once again smashed his fist into Jack's face. Jack laughed, the sound maniacal as he spit blood from his split lip. He swung the tool again, this time catching Beau across the chest in a glancing blow.

At the same time, Jack attempted to roll Beau over so that Jack would be on top. But Beau knew if that happened it would give Jack a huge advantage and right now Beau had that advantage.

As the men continued to exchange blows, Beau worried that he wouldn't be able to take control of the situation. He knew if he failed to take Jack out, then Jack would kill Peyton.

"You should have left that bitch's murder alone," Jack now yelled. "If you hadn't gone and stuck your nose in it, then I wouldn't have to kill you both now."

Jack? *Jack* had killed Lacy? He was the one who had framed Beau? In a million years Beau wouldn't have guessed Jack as the guilty party.

"Jack, you were my friend. How in the hell could you frame me for murder?" he asked.

Jack grinned up at him again from beneath where Beau sat on his chest. "You were expendable. You're nothing but swamp scum." He swung the tool again. Beau once again managed to dodge the hit.

The big man suddenly screamed and writhed against the ground. "My leg...oh, God...my leg."

Beau glanced behind him to see what had happened. Gator stood beside Jack's legs, the knife end of his walking stick buried in Jack's calf. "I definitely caught me a big one this time," the old man said with a wide grin.

Chapter Twelve

The next couple of hours flew by in a blur for Peyton. With Jack still immobile on the ground, Beau called Chief Gravois and told the lawman to bring an ambulance and meet him at the edge of the swamp by Vincent's.

She continued to cry uncontrollably, both from the pain where Jack had raked the garden tool down the side of her calf and the residual terror of what she'd just endured.

Beau left Gator in charge of Jack. "Stab him as many times as you need to in order to keep him here," Beau instructed the old man. "I'll be back with the law as soon as possible."

"Don't you worry about me," Gator said. "I've wrestled bigger beasts out here. This one isn't going anywhere."

Then Peyton was in Beau's arms. She buried her face into the crook of his neck and continued to weep as he carried her slowly out of the swamp and to Vincent's parking lot.

He continued to hold her until Gravois's car and an ambulance pulled up. Two paramedics brought a gurney over to where he stood and only then did he release her.

"Gravois, it's Jack. Jack Fontenot killed Lacy and framed Beau and he came out here to kill me," she managed to gasp amid her tears, right before she was loaded into the back of the ambulance.

She was taken to the hospital, where a doctor cleaned up and tended to the wounds on her leg. It took twenty-two stitches to close the deeper lacerations. He also cleaned up various cuts to her arms and legs from her wild dash through the swamp.

Finally, she was given a tetanus shot, pain medicine and then she was taken to a hospital bed. Left alone there, tears once again rose up inside her.

She still couldn't believe it had been Jack all along. He'd killed a young woman and betrayed his best friend, all in the name of money. It was bad enough that he'd pushed Beau out of the company, but this new information must be devastating to Beau.

Had Gravois believed what she'd said? Was Jack now in jail where he belonged? And where was Beau? How badly had he been hurt in the fight with Jack? It had been horrifying to watch the two men exchange blows.

She had so many questions and no answers. Night had completely fallen and the pain meds had begun to work, making her groggy. Would Beau come to see her? She hoped so. She desperately needed to see him, to assure herself he was okay. Surely, he cared enough about her to want to check in on her.

She fought to stay awake, waiting for him to come…needing him to come. Despite her desire to the contrary, she eventually drifted off to sleep.

Morning light drifting into the nearby window awakened her. She stirred and immediately groaned. Not only was her leg screaming in pain, but she felt like she'd been run over by a big truck. Every muscle in her body ached and she knew it was due to her sprint through the swamp.

She had almost escaped Jack the night before. She'd almost thought she was going to be able to outrun him. In the end, he'd lunged at her and caught her on the leg. If Beau had been one minute later in finding her, Jack would have succeeded in his desire to kill her.

Tears pressed hot against her eyes. They weren't tears of pain, but rather because Beau hadn't come to check on her the night before.

They were also tears of fear…maybe he couldn't come to see her. Maybe the beating he'd taken from Jack had put him someplace in this hospital.

When would somebody come in and fill her in on what had happened after she'd been whisked away by the ambulance? When would somebody come in and tell her about Beau's condition?

She'd been awake for about half an hour when a young blonde woman in lavender scrubs came in and introduced herself as Mandy.

Mandy took her vitals but had no information about anything that had happened the night before. Soon after she left Peyton's room, breakfast arrived.

She was grateful for the hot coffee, but only picked at the scrambled eggs. She had no appetite for food, but she was positively starving for information.

Her breakfast tray had just been taken away when Dr. Richards walked in. "First a gunshot wound and now this. You're keeping the emergency room busy," he said with a smile.

"No offense, but I would much prefer that the next time I see you is a social occasion and not a professional visit," she replied.

"How are you feeling?"

"A little rough," she admitted.

"I wouldn't expect anything different," he replied. "From what little I've heard you went through quite an ordeal last night."

"It was a terrible nightmare. So what happens now?"

"I'd like to keep you until after lunch, give you some more IV antibiotics and pain meds and then if you're feeling like it, we can talk about you going home sometime after lunch. That sound okay to you?"

She nodded. "That sounds fine. But can you answer a question for me?"

"Depends on what the question is," Dr. Richards replied.

"Was Beau Boudreau brought in for any treatment last night?"

"Not that I'm aware of. I can certainly tell you he isn't a patient in the hospital."

Relief fluttered in her heart. If he wasn't a patient here, then he was probably okay and that's all she'd wanted—needed—to know.

"Now, I'll get out of here and let you rest and then I'll be back around noon or so to see how you're doing," Dr. Richards said, and then he was gone. Mandy returned to administer the medicine and then Peyton was once again left alone.

She closed her eyes, and she must have dozed off, for when she opened her eyes again Beau was sitting in the chair next to her bed. He had a black eye and one side of his jaw was darkened with a bruise.

Her heart squeezed tight at the sight of him. "Oh, Beau." She only managed to get his name out and then a wave of tears overtook her.

"Peyton, don't cry. Are you hurting? Do I need to get the doctor?" he asked in alarm.

"No. I'm n-not crying because I h-hurt. I'm crying because you got hurt," she managed to say through her tears.

He leaned over and took hold of her hand. "I'm okay, Peyton. Besides, I'd fight anyone in the world to keep you safe." He squeezed her hand and then released it.

"Is Jack in jail?" she asked as her tears began to ebb.

"Not yet. He's someplace here in the hospital under armed guard. Gator's walking stick did a bit of damage to Jack's leg."

"Thank God for Gator and his trusty walking stick," she replied. "So tell me everything that happened after I was taken away."

"Jack tried to convince Gravois that we had it all wrong, that he had nothing to do with Lacy's murder. But I pointed out that Jack had come to my cabin with a weapon to kill you. Gravois started asking Jack some difficult questions and Jack finally fell apart and wound up confessing to everything. It's over, Peyton. My name has been cleared and you're free to go back to your life without worrying about any danger."

She searched his features, seeking some softness, some sense that he loved her. She thought she saw it in the very depths of his beautiful dark eyes.

"Beau, please forgive me for the mistakes I made fifteen years ago." Tears filled her eyes once again. "I'm sorry I wasn't there for you when you needed me. But I'm so deeply in love with you, Beau."

He raked a hand through his hair and released a weary sigh. "I'm in love with you, too." Her heart sang with his words. "But Peyton," he continued, "I'm not going to be your future."

"What do you mean?" Her heart immediately took a nosedive.

"I mean once you're healed up, you need to go back to the life you were living before I interrupted it," he said.

"But I don't want that life," she replied frantically. "I want the future we planned years ago. I want a future of us loving each other and living together. I want to have your babies, Beau. We can have it all now. Remember how you used to tell me I was your swamp princess? I want to be that again."

"I'm swamp, Peyton, and I'll always be swamp and you'll never be. I'd just be a hindrance to you going forward." He stood, his eyes now shuttered. "Forget about the future we once planned together. We were just kids dealing in fantasy and not reality."

"Beau…please," she cried. "I want you… I need you. I've never loved a man the way I love you."

"Eventually, you'll find the right man to love. Just forget about me, Peyton. Please, just forget about me." He didn't give her an opportunity to reply, but instead turned on his heel and left her room.

What had just happened? He'd told her he loved her, but he was walking away from her? Because he was from the swamp? Because he thought he'd be a hindrance in her life going forward?

Tears chased each other down her cheeks. He'd apparently turned all noble on her, and that ticked her off. Damn him for thinking he knew what was best for her.

She cried until she had no more tears left to cry and then she finally managed to pull herself together. Thankfully, she did, for at that moment Gravois walked into her room.

"Peyton, do you feel up to a chat?" he asked. "I need to get an official statement from you, so is this a good time?"

"It's a fine time," she replied. As he took a seat in the chair next to her bed, she raised the head of her bed so she was sitting up straighter.

"Can you start from the beginning and tell me exactly what happened last night?" he asked.

She began from the time Jack had stepped into the shanty. She told him about Jack confessing to killing Lacy and setting up Beau. Then she told him about Jack's desire to kill her in order to stop their investigation.

As she talked about the terrifying run through the swamp, tears once again burned at her eyes. "I finally tripped and that's when he caught me in the leg. Then Beau showed up and the two men fought. If Beau hadn't shown up when he did then there's no question in my mind that I'd be dead. Jack was going to tear out my throat so you'd believe it was another Honey Island killing."

When she was finished, she swiped away the tears that had leaked down to her cheeks—tears of residual fear and immense sadness over her conversation with Beau.

"Peyton, I don't even know where to begin," Gravois said. He gazed at her with sad eyes and a humbleness she'd never seen from him before. "I can't believe I got so many things wrong in my initial investigation into Lacy's death. I not only did a disservice to Beau, but also to the entire town. I would have never guessed that Jack was the guilty party in this and I'm sorry it took you getting hurt for the truth to come out."

"I'm not really the one you need to apologize to. Beau lost fifteen years of his life. He's the one who deserves an apology at the very least."

He nodded. "I'll be speaking to the town council about some sort of a monetary settlement with Beau. It's the very least I can do."

Minutes later Gravois was gone and the smell of food wafting down the hallway and into her room let her know it was lunchtime. Shortly after she was served lunch, Dr. Richards came back into her room with Mandy at his side.

"How are you feeling?" the doctor asked.

"Ready to break out of here," she replied.

"Before I let you go, we're going to take a look at your stitches and change your bandages," he said. "Then if everything looks good, I'll write you a script for antibiotics and some pain meds."

Half an hour later her bandages had been changed, her IV had been removed and she was redressed in the jean shorts and navy blue tank top she'd worn in. She'd also called Jackson for a ride home from the hospital, and she now sat on the edge of her bed to await him.

"Girl, what have you gotten yourself into this time?" he asked minutes later as he swept into her room. "I hadn't heard that you were here, otherwise I would have been here first thing this morning to check up on you. So tell me all."

"Jack Fontenot tried to kill me last night but thankfully I managed to escape with just some stitches in my leg," she replied.

"The town is all abuzz this morning about Jack's guilt in Lacy's murder. I guess you were right about Beau all along."

"Yeah, I'll try not to say 'I told you so' too many times," she replied with a wan smile.

At that moment Mandy came back into the room pushing a wheelchair. "All ready to go?"

"I'm ready." Peyton took a seat in the wheelchair while Jackson ran ahead to move his car up to the curb.

"Do you mind driving me through the pharmacy? I've got two scripts to fill," she asked once she and Jackson were on their way away from the hospital.

"No problem," he replied.

As they waited in the drive-through for her medicine, she filled him in on everything that had happened the night before. However, she didn't say anything about what had occurred earlier that morning with Beau.

"I have one more favor to ask," she said as Jackson pulled away from the drive-through window.

"Anything, my love," Jackson replied with a warm smile.

"I don't want you to drop me off at my house. I need you to drop me off at Vincent's Grocery."

Jackson shot her a sharp glance. "What are you doing, Peyton?"

"I'm not sure," she admitted. "All I know is Beau loves me and I love him. Jackson, he's my happiness and I desperately hope my future is with him. I have to go talk to him."

"For God's sake, you just got out of the hospital. You have a million stitches in your leg. Surely, this can wait."

She shook her head with determination. "No, it can't wait. I need to talk to Beau right now." Her heart beat frantically with her desperate need. Beau didn't get to just walk away from her for her own good.

Jackson sighed. "You know all I've ever wanted for you was your happiness. Far be it for me to stand in the way of true love." He turned the car and headed in the direction of the little grocery store.

"Thank you, Jackson. I want your support and I need your friendship always."

"And you'll have my friendship always," he returned. "I suppose that means I'll have to make nice with Beau in the future."

"That's a must. Honestly, Jackson, if you just give him a chance you might actually like him."

By that time Jackson had pulled into Vincent's parking lot. He parked the car, shut off the engine and then turned in his seat to gaze at her. "Do you even know your way through the swamp to get to his place?"

"I think I do." She looked toward the swamp and a bit of trepidation swept through her. "I have a general idea of where his shanty is."

"Then let's go," he said and opened his car door.

"You aren't going with me," she protested.

"I can't let you go in there all alone," he replied. "You aren't even sure where you're going."

"And you know the way?" She raised an eyebrow at him.

"Of course I don't, but I can't just let you go off all by yourself when you're obviously hurt," he replied.

"Jackson, I insist I go by myself," she said firmly. "I don't want you with me. Besides, if I get lost, I'll just yell for Beau. If he doesn't come for me, then I have a feeling Gator will find me and lead me home."

Home had become the shanty with Beau. It was where she belonged. She belonged wherever he was, and he belonged with her. She was determined to go into the darkness of the swamp to claim the love of the only man who lit her up inside.

BEAU YANKED THE sheets off his bed and tossed them into a bag to take to the laundromat. The sheets all smelled like Peyton and he refused to spend another night surrounded by her evocative scent.

He pulled out a clean set from the top of his closet and then set about remaking the bed. He'd already packed up her clothes and cosmetics into the backpack she'd initially brought with her when she'd come to heal from her shoulder wound. He'd also packed away her cell phone.

In the next day or two he'd see to it that she got all her items back. He just couldn't face doing that today. The hospital visit he'd shared with her earlier in the day had left him emotionally drained except for a deep grief.

Still, he knew he'd done the right thing in breaking things off with her. He'd already brought enough pain, both physical and emotional, to her life.

The anger he'd felt toward her in betraying him all those years ago was gone. It had died the moment he'd heard her scream when Jack had attacked her. Besides, he couldn't be angry with her for being young and malleable to the forces that had surrounded her.

Still, without that anger he was left only with his deep love for her. And it was that love that had made him leave her. He kept telling himself over and over again that it had been the right thing to do.

He was not only reeling from his breakup with Peyton. His head was still trying to wrap around the fact that it had been Jack who had murdered Lacy and set Beau up to take the fall.

The man had completely fooled Beau. Beau had grown up with Jack. They'd been friends for years, close friends, but Beau hadn't recognized the darkness that apparently lived in the man's soul.

He finished making the bed and then went into the living room and sank down in his chair. He was exhausted. The previous night had been endless, starting with Jack's arrest. After the arrest he'd first gone to the hospital to check on Peyton's condition. The doctor had told him she'd received a number of stitches in her leg but was resting comfortably.

That was all he needed to hear—that she was okay. Then he had driven to the police station to give Gravois an official statement.

It had been nearly dawn by the time he'd gotten home. He'd tried to nap, but sleep had remained elusive. Now sleep tugged at him and with a deep sigh, he surrendered to it.

He immediately fell into dreams of Peyton. Her presence and her laughter here had chased away all the dark memories of growing up with his father and the fact that his mother had abandoned him. In his dream he held her in his arms, and her beautiful blue eyes stared into his. Love. It emanated from her very being and warmed him through to his very soul.

She suddenly vanished. His arms were empty and aching with her absence. He called out her name, needing to find her. Tears burned at his eyes as he realized she was truly gone…gone forever.

"Beau…" Her voice whispered his name.

Where was she? And why was she calling his name. She needed to stay away from him.

"Beau." This time it was louder than a whisper and he suddenly jerked awake. She stood just inside the door. Her leg was wrapped up in bandages and a wrinkle that he recognized as pain etched across her forehead.

"Peyton." He jumped up out of his chair. "What are you doing here?"

"Beau, I… I need a place to heal again," she said and then burst into tears.

He quickly walked over to her and then led her to the sofa, where she collapsed. He couldn't believe she was here. He couldn't believe she'd walked through the swamp all alone with an injured leg to get to him.

She cried for several long moments and then pulled herself together. "Please don't make me leave, Beau. I need to be here with you."

Her eyes begged him and he didn't know what to do or what to say to her. He'd thought he'd said all he needed to say earlier in the day in the hospital room. So why had she come here?

"Peyton, it's obvious you're in pain. Do you have medicine to take?" He was buying time to figure out what he was going to do now that she was here.

She pulled two prescription bottles out of her pocket. "One is an antibiotic and the other is pain medicine. I'm due both."

He took the bottles from her, shook one pill out of each and then got her a glass of water. He carried the pills and the water to her. She took the pills and chased them with a big gulp of water and then set the glass on the coffee table.

"Why did you come here, Peyton? I thought I made it clear to you earlier this morning that we needed to part ways," he finally said.

"You made that decision. I didn't," she replied. "You don't get to just walk out of my life, Beau Boudreau. You don't get to decide what's good for me or not." Her chin raised defiantly and she struggled up to a sitting position.

He took several steps back from her. "It's the best decision I could make for both of us."

"That's baloney." She struggled up and got to her feet. "No matter what you say, we were destined to be together on the first night when you led me out of the swamp. You love me, Beau. I know you do, and I love you."

Tears slowly seeped from her eyes, breaking his heart all over again. *Stay strong*, he told himself. He had to stay strong but it was so damned hard when she was standing right in front of him with her love for him on full display.

"Peyton, please don't make this more difficult than it already is. Why don't you rest for a little while and then I'll take you home," he said.

"Don't you get it? This is my home." She moved closer to him. "Wherever you are is my home. We're a team, Beau. It doesn't matter that you're swamp and I'm town. It never mattered. You're my strength, the rock I can depend on to always have my back. And I'll be your strength whenever you need me to be."

Her words chipped away at his resolve. As she stepped even closer to him all his muscles tightened. "Just love me, Beau. Let me love you and give you babies and let us build the future we deserve, the one that was stolen from us by Jack."

She was now so close to him he could smell her, that scent that always dizzied his senses. "Peyton," he said in protest, but his voice sounded weak to his own ears.

"You are not any sort of a liability in my life, Beau. You are my heart and my very soul." She reached up and wound her arms around his neck. He stood stiffly in her embrace.

"You will never meet a woman who will love you as much as I do. For God's sake, do the right thing and give us a chance."

He could stand it no longer. He crashed his lips down to hers, kissing her with all the love he had in his heart for her. When the kiss finally ended, he gazed down into her eyes.

"I love you, Peyton. I love you with all my heart and soul, but I never want to be the reason you don't get business. I don't ever want to affect your life in a negative way."

"If somebody doesn't want to do business with me because my husband grew up in the swamp, then I don't want to do business with them," she said fervently.

"Husband?" He quirked an eyebrow.

"You are going to marry me, Beau Boudreau," she said with that confidence he found so sexy.

He laughed. "Yes, I'm going to marry you."

"And right now we're going to celebrate that we caught a killer and cleared your name."

"And what do you have in mind for a celebration?" he asked, even though he already knew. His entire body lit on fire as she smiled at him seductively.

"You have to be gentle with me," she whispered.

"I promise I can be very gentle." He swept her up in his arms and headed for the bedroom.

She owned his very heart, and he knew she was

his future and he was hers. Their love had been interrupted years ago, but now he was positive their future
together was bright.

Epilogue

"Come on, Beau, we need to get going," Peyton yelled from the living room into the bedroom.

"I'm coming," he replied as he walked into the room. He flashed her that slightly wicked smile that always melted her insides. He picked up the backpack on the sofa and slung it around his back. "Ready?"

"Ready," she replied. Together they left the shanty to head into town.

It had been a little over two weeks since the truth had come out about Jack's guilt and Beau's innocence. To Peyton and Beau's surprise, Beau had become something of a folk hero among the townspeople, and it had been amazing to watch him gain back his own self-respect.

They now walked through the swamp toward Vincent's parking lot. This time Peyton felt more confident about navigating through the tangled growth. Her leg was healing up nicely, although she would always bear scars from that horrible night.

They had also decided how the logistics of their

lives would work. During the week while she worked in her office, they stayed in town in her house. From Friday evening until Monday morning, they stayed in the shanty, the place they jokingly referred to now as their love shack.

"Today I should be able to finish up the painting on the office," he said once they were in his truck.

"It's already looking much nicer," she replied.

"It will look even better when it's painted a steel gray with black lettering. It will look fresh and very professional. People will be committing crimes left and right just for a chance to do business with the new and improved LaCroix Law Firm."

She laughed. "I certainly hope not. There are already enough crimes taking place around here." Her laughter died as she thought of the swamp women who had been so brutally murdered. Gravois still had nobody under arrest for the crimes.

They reached the office and together they got out of his pickup. "I'll just get to work out here and I'll see you around noon so we can have lunch together," he said.

"Before I head inside there's something I wanted to toss out to you," she said.

He grinned at her, that slow, sexy smile that made her knees weaken. "You know I'll catch whatever you throw to me." He drew her into his arms.

"I was just thinking with Jack's arrest, there's an opening for a new construction company in town," she said.

He frowned. "It's not that easy, Peyton. I don't have any start-up money for something like that. Jack was my financial backer initially and after that fiasco I'm not sure who I'd want to be my next backer."

"What about me? I have some money tucked away in my retirement account and I could use it to back you. It would be a great partnership... I provide the money and you run the business."

He stared down into her eyes. "You would do that for me?" he asked softly.

She smiled. "Don't you get it, Beau? I would do anything for you. Besides, I consider you an excellent investment."

"And I would do absolutely anything for you," he replied as his dark eyes loved her and his arms tightened around her. "I love you, Peyton."

"And I love you." She barely got the words out of her mouth before he took her lips with his in a tender kiss that spoke of deep commitment, abiding love and a beautiful future with the slightly wicked, slightly irreverent, man from the swamp.

* * * * *

Chapter One

Jackson Fortier pulled his car into one of the back parking spaces on the side of Vincent's Gas and Grocery Store. The little store was the last establishment before the vast swamp that more than half surrounded the small town of Black Bayou, Louisiana.

There were more than a dozen cars parked there as Vincent Smith, the owner of the place, allowed people who lived in the swamp to keep their vehicles there. His sleek sports car stuck out like a sore thumb amid the old model cars and banged up pickups.

It was just after noon and the late August sun was bright and cast down waves of heat. He got out of the car and pulled a note from his pocket. On the sheet of paper were directions to his best friend, Peyton, and her husband Beau's shanty.

He'd never been to their place in the swamp before. Peyton had offered to meet him here and lead him in, but he'd insisted he was a big boy and with directions he could get himself there.

However, as he stood and stared up the trail before

him, he was sorry he hadn't taken Peyton up on her offer. Tangled vines, overhanging leaves and Spanish moss made the path disappear into semidarkness.

Where the sunlight did manage to penetrate through, it shone on pools of water on either side of the path, dark waters that were filled with gators and snakes and all sort of other mysterious creatures.

The only place Jackson was at home on a trail was when he was walking the greens on a golf course. He fingered the directions in his hand as a wave of apprehension shot through him. It wasn't too late to call Peyton and have her meet him here, but he was reluctant to do so.

Surely if Peyton could traverse these paths alone, then he could as well. He glanced down at the directions. *Go straight ahead until you reach a fork. Take the path to the left.* That's all he read. He'd look at the next part when he reached the fork.

He drew a deep breath and then began to walk slowly forward. There was a distinctive odor in the air. It was a combination of something sweetly floral coupled with greenery and earthiness and the distinctive scent of decay.

Insects buzzed and clicked all around his head, creating a cacophony of sound that was totally alien to him. A rustling came from either side of him as if small creatures were running away from his presence. At least he hoped like hell they were running away from him.

The apprehension inside him rose higher as he

forged ahead, watching every single step where he placed his feet. He admitted he'd been a fool to attempt this for the first time all alone.

He could easily fall into the dark waters on either side of the path and be eaten by a gator or bitten by a venomous snake and die an agonizing death. Hell, he could get lost in the vast depths of the swamp and never be seen or heard from again.

He'd like to think the sheen of moisture that covered his skin was from the heavy humidity that hung in the air, but he suspected it was the perspiration of fear.

Hell, he could face down a shark across the table in a boardroom and beat most any man in a financial game, but walking into the swamp had him on edge like nothing he'd ever experienced before in his life.

"Suck it up, man," he said aloud to himself. He crept along at a snail's pace and dodged the low hanging branches that threatened to take his head off. He jumped and cursed as a large splash sounded far too close for comfort in the waters to his left.

He took a couple more steps, then stopped and whirled around as a rustling noise came from behind him. His heart raced and his body filled with fight-or-flight adrenaline. He saw nothing. Hopefully, it was just another little animal scurrying through the brush and not a wild boar bent on eating him.

He turned back around and took another couple of steps. The rustling came again and this time when he turned around to look, his right foot stepped off the narrow path and directly into the dark water.

A string of curses escaped him as he quickly yanked his foot up and out. Dammit, it had been stupid for him to wear his good loafers and nice black slacks. All of his clothes, including the nice shirt he had on, would probably be ruined by the end of this trek.

He stopped cursing and immediately heard the sound of musical laughter coming from someplace behind him. He whirled around again and there she was…one of the most beautiful women he had ever seen in his life.

She was clad in a pair of jeans and a white sleeveless blouse that showcased her deep tan. Long dark hair spilled down her back and her dark eyes sparked with obvious humor. "First time in the swamp, Mr. Fancy Pants?"

"What gave you that idea?" he asked with a touch of humor and a bit of embarrassment.

She laughed once again and even though he knew she was laughing at him, he couldn't take offense. He probably looked like a silly fool to anyone who had been watching him bumbling his way along. But he suddenly had other things on his mind besides his own embarrassment, like who was this beautiful woman?

"My name isn't fancy pants, but it is Jackson… Jackson Fortier. And you are?"

"Josephine Cadieux, but folks around here just

call me Josie," she replied. "What are you doing out here in the swamp? It's obvious you aren't a frequent visitor."

"Definitely not. I'm on my way to visit with friends. Maybe you know them, Peyton LaCroix and Beau Boudreau?"

"I not only know them, I'm friendly with them," she replied.

"I agreed to come for a visit today and insisted Peyton didn't have to meet me to lead the way in and instead she could just give me the directions." He held out the piece of paper he'd been clutching in a death grip in his hand.

"They are close neighbors of mine. Would you like me to take you to their place?" she asked.

"That would be great," he replied with a sigh of relief. Not only would he like her to take him in, but it would also maybe give him a chance to get to know her a little better.

Her attractiveness definitely piqued his interest. And it had been a very long time since he'd been interested in any woman. He watched as she walked in front of him. "Just follow me," she said.

He couldn't help but notice the perfect roundness of her rear end, just as he had noticed the full breasts beneath her white blouse. The jeans she wore clung to her long shapely legs. Ah, there was no question that Josie Cadieux was a real stunner.

"Watch your step here," she said as the trail narrowed.

"Thanks. So, you mentioned you're a neighbor of Peyton's. Do you have a family?" he asked.

"No, it's just me," she replied. They reached the fork in the trail and she led him to the left.

"What do you do out here?" he asked. The fact that she'd said she lived alone had further intrigued him.

"I fish. That nice piece of red snapper or catfish you ate in one of your fancy restaurants in town might have been caught by me." She stopped and turned around to look at him. Her eyes held a teasing sparkle he found enchanting. "And what do you do besides wear inappropriate clothes for a visit to the swamp?"

He laughed, delighted that she had some sass to her. "I deal in real estate," he replied. It was an understatement because he dealt in all kinds of finance. It was how he'd become wealthy…and completely bored with his life.

She turned back around and continued forward. She moved with an agility and grace he admired. He followed after her, trying to step exactly where she stepped as he dodged Spanish moss and vines that threatened to consume anyone who got too close to them.

He tried to pay attention to where they were going but it was difficult to concentrate on anything but her. "So, are you single?" he asked.

"It depends on who asks me," she replied.

"What if I'm asking?"

"I'd have to think about it."

"How long would you have to think about it?" he asked.

"I'm not sure." They took a sharp fork in the trail and a shanty appeared. "That's Beau and Peyton's place." She turned and smiled. "You have arrived safely despite your fancy clothes and stumbling start."

"That's thanks to you," he replied. "You said you were neighbors of Beau and Peyton. So, where's your place?"

"Around," she replied, and there was something in her tone that let him know he'd overstepped boundaries with the question.

"So, are you usually around the same place around the same time where I met you today on other days?" He didn't want to leave here without some opportunity to see her again. He was drawn to her and wanted to get to know her better. She was so different from all the other women he had known.

It wasn't just that she was gorgeous, but it also had to do with her obvious self-reliance and the inner strength he sensed in her. He'd never thought much about the women who lived in the swamp, other than three of them who had been in the newspaper headlines recently as murder victims.

"I could possibly be around the same place again tomorrow," she replied. Once again, a flirtatious sparkle filled her eyes. "Are you sure you want to venture out here again?"

"Definitely," he replied. "Will you know tomorrow if you're single?"

She cast him a slightly mysterious smile. "We'll see tomorrow. Enjoy your visit," she said and took several steps away from him, quickly disappearing into the darkness of the swamp.

A DARK BAG stole Josie's breath away as it fell around her head to her neck and a string pulled it tight, threatening to suffocate her. Wha-what was happening? She raised her hands to get it off her, but a hard push cast her to the ground.

With a cry, she fell forward to her hands and knees. Before she could regain her footing or figure out what was happening, she was rolled over on her back.

Immediately, somebody was on top of her, grabbing her wrists and attempting to tie them together. She tried to fight back, but he managed to tie her wrists together anyway.

Shock and fear shot through her. Was this the person who had killed three women? Was she about to become the fourth victim of the Honey Island Swamp Monster?

Josie came awake and jerked up to a sitting position, her heart pounding a thousand beats a minute as sobs ripped from the very depths of her.

Looking around the bedroom with the aid of a shaft of moonlight that danced in through the nearby window, she tried to center herself. It had not only been a horrible nightmare, but it had been what had happened to her a little over ten months ago.

It took her several moments and then she managed to stop crying. She swiped the last of her tears away and then slid her legs over the side of the bed and got up. She went into the living area and lit a couple of kerosene lanterns that were on a shelf. She could have started her generator and flipped on an electric light, but it was too much trouble and, in any case, she often preferred the softer glow of the lanterns.

There was no way she was ready to go back to sleep, not with the taste of the nightmare still bitter on her tongue and thick in her chest.

She went to her front door, unlocked it and then stepped outside on the narrow porch that encircled her shanty. The sounds of the swamp surrounded her…the throaty bellow of frogs and the slap of fish in the water. Insects buzzed and clicked in a nightly chorus and there was also the rustling of night creatures as they scampered along through the nearby brush.

She'd never been afraid in the swamp. It was her home. From a young age, her parents had taught her the good plants and the bad, the things to be afraid of and the places to avoid.

No, she'd never been afraid in the swamp until that night when she'd been violated and even then, it hadn't been anyone from the swamp.

The man who had raped her had been from town. His hands had been far too soft to be anyone from the swamp. He'd smelled of expensive cologne and even though he'd only spoken a few words to her, she knew she would never ever forget the sound of his deep voice.

She'd immediately reported the assault to the chief of police, Thomas Gravois. She knew if she'd been a young woman from town, Gravois would have moved heaven and earth to solve the crime. But because she was from the swamp, next to nothing had been done about it.

That didn't mean she was just going to forget about it. One way or another, she intended to find the man and expose him. However, there was a huge obstacle standing in her way.

As a woman from the swamp, she had no invite into the inner circle of wealthy men that ran the town of Black Bayou. And she believed with all her heart that was where her personal monster hid.

She thought about the man she had led in to Peyton and Beau's place. The minute she'd seen him, she'd known who he was. Jackson Fortier was one of the most eligible single men in the small town. He was not only wickedly handsome, but he was also extremely wealthy.

Josie didn't give a damn about his money, but he could potentially be an entry into where she wanted to go. Or she could possibly never see him again.

One thing was certain, he wasn't the man who had attacked her. She'd know the sound of her attacker's voice and Jackson wasn't him.

With the nightmare finally behind her and the lullaby of the swamp soothing her, she went back inside and returned to her bed. She stared up at her dark ceiling and finally sleep claimed her once again.

She awakened just after sunrise. She dressed quickly and went out her back door where a pirogue was tied up. The small boat was what she used to check the lines that she'd baited the night before.

She added her push pole and an oar, along with her tackle box, and then she got into the pirogue and used the push pole to glide slowly away from her home.

Mornings in the swamp were positively magical as far as she was concerned. The sunlight dappled the glistening water with gold tones and birds sang from the treetops. Fish jumped high, as if rested by the night and now eager to show off their prowess.

There was a peace here, a reassurance that the ecosystem was working the way it should and all was well. She glided across the water, barely making a ripple as she used her paddle only when it was necessary.

Josie didn't need to make a lot of money. She paid no rent and had no utility bills. But she did need money for the gas she put in her generator to give her a little electricity when she wanted it. Just like any other twenty-seven-year-old, she liked to occasionally buy a new outfit for herself, although she had few places to go where anyone might admire her choice of fashion.

Most of the time, her money went into a large jug

she kept in the closet in her bedroom. It had grown to be a healthy savings account, although she had no idea what she was saving it for.

Many of the women she knew were saving their money so they could, somehow, someday escape the swamp. Josie had never really had a desire to leave this place that was in her heart and very soul. There had just been two times when she'd wished things might have been different, but she didn't want to think about those times now.

She reached the place where her fishing lines were located and began to pull them up. She was eager to discover what had been caught overnight.

An hour later, she was heading home, pleased with her catch of the day. When she reached her shanty, she placed the fish she'd caught into a cage she had in the water. They would stay alive until she had enough caught to take them into town and sell.

Once the fish were squared away, she started her generator and went back into the house. Her parents had worked hard to make their shanty as updated as possible.

The generator not only provided electricity for lights and small appliances, but also a heated water system for showering. The only thing they hadn't been able to have was a working refrigerator. So, every couple of days, Josie went to Vincent's and bought ice and a few items to keep in a large ice chest.

Although she did much of her cooking on top of the potbelly stove, there were mornings when it was too warm, or she just didn't want to go to the trouble to build a fire.

She now plugged in a single burner cooktop and the toaster. She then got two eggs out of her cooler along with a stick of butter.

Minutes later, she sat at the small table in the kitchen area to eat. It was at this time when she missed her parents the most. The three of them had always eaten breakfast together. They'd talk about the day to come and share happy laughter. Unfortunately, her father had passed two years ago from cancer and her mother had followed him six months later and died from a massive heart attack.

The past year and a half had been lonely for Josie, although soon after her mother's passing, she'd thought she'd met the man of her dreams. Even though he'd been a town guy, she'd been certain their love story had been written in the stars. She'd been so wrong and that experience had taught her a valuable lesson.

She washed up her dishes and then went in for a quick shower. As she stood beneath the warm spray of water, she wondered if Jackson would really show up today. She intended to be there just in case he did, but she wouldn't be surprised if he didn't come.

After showering, she changed into a pair of capri jeans and a hot-pink sleeveless blouse that she knew looked good on her. It always took her a few minutes to brush through her long hair. Normally, she didn't wear makeup, but today she put on a little mascara and then spritzed on her favorite perfume.

Just beneath the waistband of her jeans, she tucked in a sheath that carried a small but wickedly sharp knife. Since her assault, she never left the house without the weapon. She would never be caught utterly defenseless again.

By then it was time for her to leave. She grabbed her key to the front door, shoved it in a pocket and then left the shanty.

An edge of excitement raced through her as she headed back to the place where she had first seen Jackson the day before. A smile curved her lips as she remembered watching him bumble his way into the swamp.

Even though he'd been very tentative and she'd found him slightly comical, there was no question that he was a hot hunk.

His dark hair had looked thick and rich and his bright blue eyes had been unexpected yet beautiful. His facial features were strong and bold and wonderfully handsome. Even beneath his fancy lavender shirt, she could tell his shoulders were broad and his waist was slim. Oh, yeah, definitely a hunk.

If he did show up today, then it would mean he was interested in her. And if she played her cards right with him, then she might be welcomed into the wealthy inner circle and she'd potentially be able to identify her assailant.

If she didn't like Jackson, she'd pretend she did

anyway. If she did like him then it would certainly make things easier for her. No matter what happened, she wouldn't lose sight of the reality that she intended only to use him for a little while to get what she wanted…what she needed, and that was justice.

She might pretend to have a romantic interest in him, but she wouldn't allow herself to catch any real feelings for him or any other man from town. That had been the lesson she'd learned after her past relationship. She'd been there, done that, and her heart would remain closed forever.

She finally reached the spot where she'd seen Jackson the day before. She was early. As she waited to see if he'd show up, a new rush of excitement filled her. She was putting herself out there as bait and all she was hoping for now was that Jackson would take the bait and run with it.

Don't miss
Monster in the Marsh
by Carla Cassidy,
available February 2024 wherever
Harlequin Intrigue books and
ebooks are sold.

www.Harlequin.com

#2193 COLD CASE IDENTITY
Hudson Sibling Solutions • by Nicole Helm

Palmer Hudson has a history of investigating cold case crimes. Helping his little sister's best friend, Louisa O'Brien, uncover the truth about her biological parents should be simple. But soon their investigation becomes a dangerous mystery...complicated by an attraction neither can deny.

#2194 MONSTER IN THE MARSH
The Swamp Slayings • by Carla Cassidy

When businessman Jackson Fortier meets Josie Cadieux, a woman who now lives deep in the swamp, he agrees to help find the mysterious man who assaulted her a year earlier. Soon, Josie's entry into polite upper-crust society to expose the culprit changes Jackson's role from investigator to protector.

#2195 K-9 SECURITY
New Mexico Guard Dogs • by Nichole Severn

Rescuing lone survivor Elena Navarro from a deadly cartel attack sends Cash Meyers's bodyguard instincts into overdrive. The former marine—and his trusty K-9 partner—will be damned if she falls prey a second time...even if he loses his heart keeping her safe.

#2196 HELICOPTER RESCUE
Big Sky Search and Rescue • by Danica Winters

After a series of strange disappearances, jaded helicopter pilot Casper Keller joins forces with Kristin Lauren, a mysterious woman involved in his father's death. But fighting the elements, sabotage and a mission gone astray may pale in comparison to the feelings their reluctant partnership exposes...

#2197 A STALKER'S PREY
West Investigations • by K.D. Richards

Actress Bria Baker is being stalked. And her ex, professional bodyguard Xavier Nichols, is her best hope for finishing her movie safely. With Bria's star burning as hot as her chemistry with Xavier, her stalker is convinced it's time for Bria to be his...

#2198 THE SHERIFF'S TO PROTECT
by Janice Kay Johnson

Savannah Baird has been raising her niece since her troubled brother's disappearance. But when his dead body is discovered—and unknown entities start making threats—hiding out at officer Logan Quade's isolated ranch is their only chance at survival...and her brother's only chance at justice.

Get 3 FREE REWARDS!

We'll send you 2 FREE Books plus a FREE Mystery Gift.

FREE Value Over **$20**

Both the **Harlequin Intrigue®** and **Harlequin® Romantic Suspense** series feature compelling novels filled with heart-racing action-packed romance that will keep you on the edge of your seat.